Praise for *Under the Frog*

A *New York Times Book Review*
Notable Book of the Year (1993)
Runner-up for the Booker Prize (1993)

"A delicate seriocomic treasure."

—Salman Rushdie

"Brilliant. . . . *Under the Frog* is fully a work of dynamic historical imagination . . . with some spectacular scenarios and unforgettable figures. . . . Fischer writes in a comic spirit of funky, horny alienation."

—*The New York Times Book Review*

"A ferociously funny, bitterly sad, and perfectly paced account of Hungary in the 1950s."

—A. S. Byatt

"A clever, humane, and original book. . . . I wish someone would make a film of it."

—*The Times* (London)

Praise for *The Thought Gang*

"An intelligent, thoughtful black comedy."
—*The New York Times Book Review*

"Hilarious and brainy."

—*The Village Voice*

"A delicious novel, confirming Tibor Fischer as one of the most brilliant novelists of his generation."

—*Daily Telegraph* (London)

"This brilliant improvisation is really a sexual interpretation of the history of Western thought. . . . It deserves to become a cult novel for the 1990s."

—*The Times* (London)

THE

COLLECTOR
COLLECTOR

THE
COLLECTOR
COLLECTOR

a novel by
TIBOR FISCHER

METROPOLITAN BOOKS
HENRY HOLT AND COMPANY
NEW YORK

Metropolitan Books
Henry Holt and Company, Inc.
Publishers since 1866
115 West 18th Street
New York, New York 10011

Metropolitan Books™ is an imprint of
Henry Holt and Company, Inc.

Published in Canada by Fitzhenry & Whiteside Ltd.,
195 Allstate Parkway, Markham, Ontario L3R 4T8.

Library of Congress Cataloging-in-Publication Data
Fischer, Tibor.
  The collector collector / Tibor Fischer.—1st ed.
    p. cm.
  I. Title.
PR6056.I772C6   1997   96-44330
823'.914—dc20   CIP

ISBN 0-8050-5118-X

Henry Holt books are available for special
promotions and premiums. For details contact:
Director, Special Markets.

First Edition—1997

Designed by Paula R. Szafranski

Printed in the United States of America
All first editions are printed on acid-free paper.∞
          1 3 5 7 9 10 8 6 4 2

Eszternek

And they gave unto Jacob all the strange gods which were in their hand and all their earrings which were in their ears, and Jacob hid them under the oak. . . .

GENESIS 35.4

I've had a planetful.

Impending owner: old, obese, oooooorotund. Only one hundred and one hairs for his barber to worry about. Jowly. Flesh dripping off his face, melted by age. Balloon. A fat-filled balloon. His belt is nearly longer than he is. Lugal. Lugal number ten thousand four hundred and sixty twoooooo.

"Smedley will be in touch with you," he says.

Present holder: auctioneeress. She sells the world the world. Red cotton from India under ruffled blue tweed. Ten denier stockings. Tomato-red lipstick. An expert with one child; she has rigid thighs where big men have whimpered like small dogs, but she is still lonely.

"I thought you only used him to sue members of your own family," she replies.

Lugals aren't strong on humor. Power rarely has a use for humor. They don't have much interest in being entertaining or popular. This one tries to act as if he does: a project perhaps to help him imagine that people are drawn to him for his charm and wit and not his integrity-crushing riches. There are lugals like that.

"No. No. Not just that." He exposes twenty-three percent of his teeth as a smile. "That's if all the checks verify it's genuine."

Genuine? The genuine ones don't look as good as me. I'm better than genuine. I'm the original, so genuine, the genuine ones look like copies—which, of course, is what they are.

"I have a good feeling about this," she says.

"And you'll use Rosa?"

"I'm going straight to Rosa's."

"Good. I have a lot of faith in Rosa. A lot of faith."

Street: paved. Called King. W.1. London. England. It's been two thousand and sixteen years since I've been near the Thames. Can't say I've missed it, though I could lead you to some fascinating burial sites. Surroundings don't matter much to me. Everything's been under or near a river. Rivers, if you watch patiently enough, flicker and jag like slow, dull lightning. Water, like a lumbering drunk, has pissed and slouched all over this planet.

"It's going to rain," he says, quite concerned. There is one tiny, feeble cloud in view. With the information available to me, I would reckon the odds on rain in the next hour as 5,000 to 1 against.

"If I get caught in the rain, I bleed," he says in a tone that is aiming to hook sympathy.

She nods, slightly oddly. He probably interprets this as sympathy because that's what he wants, so he can take a little odd-looking sympathy. I, on the other hand, interpret it as the auctioneeress biting the inside of her mouth to stop herself from laughing, because he is, in addition to being a lugal, a clown, a multi-story car park filled with jalopies of laughability, soooooo preposterous, a baboon of prodigious risibility; I adjust his position from the early ten thousands to bring him up to just outside the supreme thousand, though I am well aware that if I am in his company for much longer, he will penetrate the supreme hundred laughingstocks. Of my collectors, he is already the most mockable.

The auctioneeress looks up to the sky as if pondering its cruelty, but more likely to give her teeth the chance to hang on to her cheeks. He is, to the core, a lugal, loaded. He has lots of money; she doesn't. And while he might feel obliged to take some ribbing, outright contempt might sour relations. She needs the money, otherwise she wouldn't be conducting an unauctioned sale for a backhander. Child-thinking-of. Her lips have the unmistakable pursing of someone with much knowledge and little chance of making money. So much and yet so little, that is what she is thinking.

With all my medical experience—greater than any three teaching hospitals you could care to name—I have never detected a condition where drops of rain can be traded for drops of blood. And besides which, it is a mark of the lugal that whatever their quirks, they bounce like balls. You can drop them from a great height, dump them into a volcano, clobber them with a whale. They never tire in loofahing their egos and feeding them grapes. No lugal ever perished in drizzle.

He signals to a car waiting down the street. It is a vehicle fit for a lugal, a limousine with smoked windows so that he need not be sullied by passersby's gazes.

"I don't like taking the car. Cars are nothing but metal missiles hunting each other down on the roads. Huge metal monsters hurtling at each other. Designed to kill as much as a gun. Crazy invention." He is getting panicky; he has to walk to the car and thus expose himself for eight feet to the risk of rain, and his ear wiggling betrays the thought that once he reaches the car, he will be signing up for the risk of a pile-up. The great pity about the absurdly rich is that they become absurd because none of them have the foresight to buy a wanker alarm, someone who would accompany them and just toll at apposite moments: "You are being soooooo wanky." That is the danger of wild wealth, it frees you from gravity. They could hire the poor for the job. They'd have to be changed every so often like batteries, because their good sense would be dissipated in the plush restaurants and chichi boutiques.

"You're so lucky not to have money. So lucky," he says, the foreignness in his diction rising from eighteen percent to a peak of twenty-nine. "When you have money people are simply after you, all the time. All the time. You know, I have seven teams of accountants working for me. The second checks the first, the third checks on the second, the fourth checks on the third. And so on. The first also check on the seventh. And even if they're not stealing, they might as well be for the fees they charge. And as for my family . . . there's no end to it. This bowl is just what I want."

"So why are you looking so miserable?"

"I'm afraid it's a trick to get my money. Someone must have heard I want one for my collection."

"You can give me some of your money, Marius."

"I wouldn't wish it on you. And what can you do with it? Banks go bankrupt. Companies go bust. Even top-notch banks in top-notch economies go kablooey. Civilizations drop dead like flies. There's no safety. You have to watch all the time. You have no idea how bad it is. Say hello to Rosa for me."

You could take his words and grind them down to quarks and you wouldn't find the slightest trace of irony. I have now slotted him in at number one hundred and fifteen. He waddles off, his gait topped up with ridiculousness by the gold ingots he is carrying under his shirt. Gold, the shining

4

shunner, so beloved of the rich and the poor, play-fellow of
the learned, so ungiving of itself. I wonder why he doesn't
employ someone to carry the fire extinguisher he has grasped
in his left hand.

The auctioneeress and I get into a rickety car and drive
south, across the river. "Why?" she asks. "Why?"

She says this sixteen times on our journey, the word roller-
coasting from bitterness to amusement. A prime timeburster.
In the index of the billions of vocalizations I have catalogued,
this is the import that occurs most often. A sound that's been
around, too. Unripe apples here, soul's sigh there. If you wait
long enough, any word or sound gets to mean everything.

But I can't help her with her inquiry.

Rosa

Everything. Been it. Seen it. Mean it.

You think you've had a demonstrably hard time? Your
job, let me guess, is made of solid odium?

Now, I've been *used*: abused, disabused, misused, mused
on, underenthused, unamused, contused, bemused, and even
perused. Any compound of used, but chiefly used: shaving
bowl, vinegar jar, cinerary urn, tomb good, pyxis, vase, rat-
trap, krater, bitumen amphora, chamber pot, pitcher, executioner, doorstop, sunshade, spittoon, coal scuttle, parrot rest,
museum exhibit, deity, ashtray. If you're quiet, don't fuss
and take it, it's staggering what people will dump on you. If
it's vile, I've had a pile—*and* I know more than five thousand
languages (even if you want to get dainty about what's a language and what isn't).

She puts me down on a low table, folds her arms, and
looks down at me sternly.

"Talk," she commands.

This is an idiotic, if not deranged thing, to say to a bowl, even to a bowl like me, thin-walled, sporting the scorpion look of Samarra ware that was the rage of Mesopotamia six and a half thousand years before Rosa was born. Pottery, after all, isn't renowned for its chatty nature, so why futilely address a vessel thus—even me, the bowl with soul? But Rosa is far from being unhinged.

Inevitably, I've been talked to, more than anyone would credit. Being inanimate doesn't earn you any dispensation from being buttonholed. People prefer people, will accept pets, but failing all else, they will unburden themselves to the crockery. And, naturally, supplied with sonic tools, I could chatter. I could chatter until this young lady, her flat, and her city were nothing but unremarkable dust.

I'm not sure what's going on here. Lately I stick to collectors of note. Moneybags. Lugals. Those deformed by excessive wealth, those who will lay down reverence all around me. The trials of being a utensil didn't bother me for a long time, but I've become soooooo tired of indignity, of some dullard keeping terrapins or busy lizzies in me.

Reverence is my quarry, and giving a hint of my pedigree achieves this, age and a dash of the flash equalling venerability in the pottery game. Old? How old? Oooooold. Old before old was invented.

Does this make me a snob? Yes, I do like my collectors destructively rich and obeisant. Granted, the oofy are goofy, the disgustingly rich are often disgusting, but that's an epithet that doesn't turn up its nose at escorting those who have only moderate amounts of money and those who have none.

Rosa: cordial, respectful, relaxed.

She is, I educe, some expert, scrutinizing me; this is

because my last few carriers have been poorly presented individuals from a region not enjoying a reputation for probity or rectitude or any of the qualities that make a buyer feel better about a transaction—especially when it comes to pottery worth a lottery.

The vogue for savants is white coats and frowns, slipping some solemnity under their métier to raise its importance. They like props: gauges, drills, beakers. Their investigations don't fluster me; if you have no idea what you're looking for, you're not going to find it.

Rosa's home appears to be her place of work. She doesn't blend in with the scrutineers I have encountered. There are a few books, nowhere near enough to suggest outstanding scholarly competence, and as she grades me, she wears only minimal black underwear, which would, in isolation, be deemed unprofessional in most professions, unworkable in most workplaces.

She scratches the small of her back with her left thumbnail and then, straightening herself, places her hands on my sides. But this is entirely different from her grip on me before. I'm not expecting this.

She's live.

This is a touch I've never experienced before; it is much more than a touch.

Imagine you've been living alone for a long time and suddenly you hear the door open when it shouldn't, you hear footsteps in your bedroom where you know there shouldn't be any. A light comes on by itself, your clothes fall off by themselves, a breeze trespasses. For the first time, I know what it is to be naked.

She's through, she can hear me. Rosa's in.

Fooled. But this is only the four hundred and twelfth time.

She isn't a catalogue turner, a contour crawler, a holder of a magnifying glass. Rosa is a silence taker. A diviner. A vase tickler. An intruder.

Diviners—like everyone, I've heard about them, but to be frank, I've never been much convinced about their trade. Before Rosa, the tally of my dealings with those ostensibly having abilities to receive the hidden: three. A former rope maker in the Indus valley, a footman in Siam, and a color explorer.

As to my dealings with those purporting to have abilities to receive the hidden but who were flimming the flam, they number one hundred twenty thousand, four hundred and forty-two. The youngest being an eight-year-old shaman who had his head kicked in after his tribe had everything they owned washed away in a flash flood scouring their encampment—an encampment decreed by the shaman. The oldest was a ninety-two-year-old fortune teller in Byzantium who had been predicting winners in the chariot races for seventy-five years and had never got it right once. However, the perfection of his errors established, after twenty years he became greatly patronized by the gamblers, since his choice, while not a shortcut to winnings, could be used to eliminate one element from their calculations.

As for the true soothsayers: The ex–rope maker had been much in demand at the more vulgar celebrations at that juncture when modesty and decorum have been wholly dissolved, when, using his chosen agent of insight, his tongue, he would muzzle himself with the nautch girls and then delve into mysteries such as their places of birth, their fathers' occupations, their earliest memories, their favorite colors, their dearest aspirations, the names of their closest friends, their most-loved jewelry; the answers to which, garnered solely from his bridle of legs, earned him unbridled applause. Notwithstanding his redoubtable gift, I have to remark that the same information could well have been obtained by anyone using tools such as civil conversation and the odd bauble.

The footman: could always guess, unerringly, when it would rain. This gained him a popularity with many street traders and hunters, but he was never invited (in the bounds of my knowledge) to any rousing debauchery. A pity he couldn't boost himself from the status of rainteller to the more lucrative level of rainmaker (twenty-two bona fide on board, nineteen dubious, four hundred and ninety-eight frauds).

The Best Rainmaker

She came to the thorp near Colonia, where there hadn't been rain for nearly a year. The people were seven-eighths starved. The second n on their extinction was being fixed on.

"I will make rain," she proposed. "But only if the men of my choice make love to me for three days. Then I will make rain for three days." There was skepticism, mixed with a willingness from the venerous of the thorp, until she gave a free ten-minute sampler, bringing down rain within a three-mile circle of the place. Some of the women were unhappy about this arrangement, but the men did their duty. Afterward, having smoothed down her skirt, she brought rain: a few puny drops first, then a steady downpour, and finally a storm so powerful that even unfornicated-out men could not have stood in the deluge. The ground grew mollified, barrels brimmed, puddles ponded, rivers started to prowl. The rain stopped exactly seventy-two hours, twenty minutes, and twelve seconds after it started, perhaps reflecting the fuller's extra efforts to make sure the three-day mark had been passed.

"This is great, but we haven't had rain for nearly a year, and who knows when it'll rain again? How about another barter?" The same covenant was agreed. Some of the women had to help out since the men were so etiolated and emaciated by drought and fornication that they were good for nothing. Drops with no stops for seventy-six hours, perhaps reflecting a discount for repeat custom.

She was about to leave to locate more parched territory when they stopped her and confided: "Supreme pleasure, gratitude for the rain, but you are undeniably in league with the Evil One, so we're going to have to burn you. This is very difficult for us."

They tied her to a stake, but they had trouble lighting the kindling since it was raining rivers. "Couldn't we just hit her over the head?" It rained for six days, so heavily people couldn't see more than three feet in front of themselves. The rain stopped not long after the rainmaker drowned along with the slower, frailer, and less wanted inhabitants of the thorp. A lake, whose waters were long claimed to be noxious, cleaved to the spot for many years until I was fished out. The fifth least propitious fishing out I have endured. . . . Enough.

The Vase Tickler

Rosa's caught me unguarded, she's unblind in my mind. I've never even thought about guarding, but Rosa progresses slowly enough for me to shield myself with one of my suitable pasts. . . .

I do: a genial stretch of sunny Sumer on a good day, the day of a public execution, myself a lowly utensil, open wide to serve, a family retainer retaining the evening meal, a delegation of local smells and colors, the bickering of the fish friers. A distant lugal.

10

I do: circularity.

I do: utensiling along.

Yesteryearing with an uncommon vengeance, I become this shred of antiquity because disguise has been my custom, and because if she tapped into the full me, her brains would shoot out of her nose.

To the ninety-one types of surprise I have identified, I now have to add a new branch—that of the thinking ceramic caught naked for the first time in millions of years, in a two-bedroom flat in an inexpensive part of South London.

"You original you," Rosa proclaims, letting go of me, visibly satisfied with the platter of ur-Ur I rustled up. She is glowing after her stroll in a bowl. Her infiltration of my being has been an effort for her, which is pleasing since I wouldn't like her to make a habit of feeling my feelings. She can only hold her breath in ancient depths for a few minutes.

She scopes me, but looking at me will tell you nothing; it is her touch I fear, her hands which can finger me. She toys with her tourmaline in helical silver earrings, which signify a common story operating under numerous aliases: the lone swordsman holding the pass. She doesn't know this, but she senses it.

For irises, there are ten thousand, nine hundred and forty-nine principal hues. Rosa has mostly the gray I term mullet gray. She is probably assigning me a price (she works for the auctioneeress, so she must know how much money it takes to stop a bowl with my features).

I do the same for her. Rosa. Twenty-six. In voguish measurements, five foot four, one hundred twenty-five pounds. Hair, of the fifty-two shades of chestnut, she has what I term Genoese. On the block she wouldn't fetch a great price, men needing some drastic beauty or the likelihood of near fatal pleasure to throw their gold. Rosa's qualities of warmth and humor would not grasp the buyers' looks, though no doubt in the cold and dark, those semi-simian creatures would welcome the comfort of her hugs.

She goes off to paint pictures of the past on the back of her eyelids, inviting darkness into the room where I have now been stationed, a bare, unfurnished cube, a cell for the interrogation of ceramics.

In the ajarness of her bedroom door facing me she is squeezed into a column of light, where she dismisses her attire. Of bosom, there are two hundred and twenty styles; of buttocks, two hundred and eighty-four. I order. I know. I do my job. Her navel is type sixty-seven of two thousand, two hundred, and thirty-four, the buried bald man.

To date I have catalogued twenty-five assorted dirt pushers, nineteen unknowns, fifteen herdsmen, fourteen warriors, ten maids, nine seamstresses, seven bakers, six strumpets, five cooks, five members of the nobility or lugalling classes, three discoboli, three singers, three users of ink, two ferrymen, two flute players, two lace makers, two monarchs, two slaves, two wine scientists, a beacon minder, a carrier-home of drunken revelers, a chandler, a collector of barbed wire, a dolmen fixer, a fowler, a henna maker, a martyr, a mateotechnist, a meresman, a nothing, an oryctologist, an ostreger, a peacock breeder, a reproofer of vice, a rubber of backs, a sambuca builder, a seller of ribbons, and a sutler who have possessed this navel. It is one of my favorites. My view disappears in a burst of blackness.

Blackness sprawls everywhere; the lesser household sounds beneath daytime hearing now reach their moment of audibility. The inanimate, with the help of night, can move over to the other team. Wardrobes groan and tut, chairs flinch, floorboards fidget. I take the readings.

Two hours and fifty-three minutes elapse. The buzzer then fires a slumber-clearing missile of jagged sound, jarring even for jars.

Rosa, hunched under the weight of sleep, sways slowly to the intercom.

"Hello?" She summons all her powers to make the word.

"It's Nikki. Sorry to be so late."

"You've got the wrong flat," Rosa responds.

"Is that Rosa? Didn't Cornelia talk to you?"

Springy steps in the hallway and the newcomer is admitted. I catch a slice of her. Diminutive, lithe, carrying her rucksack with verve. No more than a few months either side of her thirtieth year. Still hoping for one hundred and sixty-seven, I find that Nikki's nose fits into the one hundred sixty-six classes I have already identified. It's number eighty-eight or the begonia. It's the nose I used for a depiction of Laïs when I was forming a black-figure vase in the style of what everyone currently calls the school of the Gorgon painter (school of me, naturally).

Nikki carries the load of the road. She explains how she has come straight from Spain, hitching. A touch of foreign heat still radiates from her. I sense that Rosa, annoyed and sleepy as she is, relishes these wisps of adventure.

Nikki apologizes, says she can't understand why Cornelia, their acquaintance in Vienna, didn't clear her arrival with Rosa. She apologizes a lot, a quite embarrassing amount, but one of the things she doesn't apologize for is lying. There are ninety-one ways of telling the truth, and this isn't number ninety-two. This is number fifty-nine of the two hundred and ten ways of lying, the technique I like to call the wild strawberry.

Concerned with regaining her bed, burrs of Ur still clinging around her, lacking my authority on untruths and

13

simply not that fussed, Rosa shows Nikki the spare room and hands her some bedding.

"How long can I crash here?" asks Nikki, well aware that the question will be shooed away for the moment, obtaining a fair reprieve. We are in the presence of an operator whose oooooonly truth so far has been her name.

Nikki at Rosa's

Light alights on the city. Rosa debeds and days herself, making no attempt to thwart the sounds of her preparation, but Nikki doesn't emerge from her room, no doubt influenced by the belief that no chance of conversation means no chance of conversation about when she moves on.

Leaving a note with the prominently placed breakfast items, Rosa departs. After counting off five minutes (in case Rosa might return for a forgotten item or might pull the pretending-to-return-for-a-forgotten-item ploy) Nikki attacks the kitchen and tucks in with the special appetite people reserve for other people's food. This is not merely breakfast with shoddy mass-produced crockery, this is storage. She works through the croissants and cold cuts, stalling on a jar of pickled beetroot whose lid won't budge. Then she starts rummaging through the flat, rushing for those nooks where you would expect the most personal and blush-making items to be; she is flipping disappointedly through a diary when the buzzer goes.

In a resident's manner, Nikki attends to the intercom, listens to the voice, peers momentarily out the window that gives her a glimpse of the caller, mutters "Four minutes," then admits a black woman, twenty-two, dressed like a saleswoman, carrying seven copies of a magazine, wanting to talk

14

about security, slightly taken aback at being invited in, as overcast Tuesday mornings usually find people unreceptive to an explanation of the universe's purpose.

Not the most skilled of mind flavorers, she launches into her prepared evangelism, clanking her sentences like ill-fitting armor; Nikki makes no interruption but mounts a thin smile.

Four minutes, twelve seconds after she entered the property, the Jehovah's Witness's clothing starts to be removed. At six minutes, nine seconds her clothing covers only the carpet. I educe that the Witness doesn't protest much, owing to the speed and surprise of the feat. Things she has never imagined and may well never have heard of are taking place—with vehemence; and indubitably, the suggestion of pleasure and pleasure itself are two different commodities to rebuff. Perhaps there should have been illustrations in the Bible to make it clear what's on and what's not.

In this year, in this topos, the Witness is not of such beauty that photographers would be handing her their cards in the street. Of the six hundred and forty forms of allure, nevertheless plainness makes up twenty of them.

Nikki: wiry. She has been either a dancer, a gymnast, an accomplished swimmer, or had a very active outdoor youth. Slight with bite. Her body is her office. An eater of small pieces of fruit, a nibbler of grain unless the food is at someone else's expense. She is the one who dodges plagues, endures sieges, comes out of the jungle, crawls from burning wreckage, who chatters longest in frozen waters.

The Witness is turned about by Nikki as if she were a blouse that needed intricate ironing; very reminiscent of a scene I adopted that got me purchased by a collector in Luxembourg and resulted in my being locked in a safe, the dread

15

of any serious work of art (and how baffled and furious he was when I deformed and dedesigned in the dark, emerging as the dullest Wedgwood I could imagine).

With equal dispatch Nikki repackages the dazed evangelist and bundles her oooooout of the door. Fifty-nine minutes, the lot. Practice. For one of Vanity's true troopers.

A long bath, long phone calls to places a long way off deal with most of the afternoon. Nikki does two loads of laundry in the washing machine, the items from her rucksack and person being so grimy that they are able to stand without the aid of a body. She counts out her money from a pouch. I make it seven pounds thirty-three pence and a hundred peseta note.

The washing machine kicks the bucket during the second load. Nikki sucks on the spectacle of the defunct machine for a while.

But Rosa takes the news of domestic disruption lightly when she returns.

Cup of Tea: One

Rosa seems to have only a caretaker consciousness to respond to Nikki's chatter. The apologies niagra out.

"I'm so sorry. Everything just . . . goes wrong," Nikki says. "Everything I do . . . I . . . I . . . I . . ." Her words transmute into a soft whine. Her face topples forward into her lap. She knows the value of tears striking the hard surface of a kitchen floor. I have seen women cry gently like this over a billion times. I decided to stop counting on the fourth of May, 1216. Certain things go on: the plying of drinks to aspired-to lovers, women's tears. Nikki is clever enough to be more inventive; Rosa is intelligent enough to spot a ruse. Just because the dull know about it, doesn't mean it doesn't work. No trick is so old it loses its efficacy.

"This is awful. . . . I'm being an awful nuisance. . . . Give me a few minutes and I'll be off."

But naturally, Nikki stays on to purvey lorries of sorries and then ranks of thanks when Rosa offers her continued shelter. Nikki drags into the kitchen fitfully, slowly, like a stubborn dog not very keen on being dragged, the holey story of why she is destitute and how she attempted suicide.

Rosa has to shoo away the truth: "I'm being a pain in the arse." "I shouldn't burden you with this." "I should go." Nikki's fiction is like her, lean and supple. She lies without effort, like a seam of anthracite, cool, deep. She, judging from the other people-surfers I have encountered, would only consider taking her life in circumstances of the most outrageous pain.

Sobs on. A failed bar in Spain, savings vaporized, a swine in the form of a man, beatings and extra-Nikki use of his manhood. Sobs off.

"So what's your job?" asks Nikki, shifting her campaign from the heart to the head.

"Art consultant," says Rosa. Nikki oooooos her eyes to show her admiration and to express how lucky Rosa is to have such a job. Her approval would have been as fierce if Rosa had declared her trade to be street sweeper or chicken gutter.

"What's that all about?"

"I authenticate works of art. If someone finds a painting or any work of art that looks a bit suspect, I'm brought in to see whether it's genuine, what period it's from, and so on."

"That sounds fantastic."

"You get to meet some interesting bowls."

"And how do you get a job like that?"

"I started off as a secretary in an auction house. Then you . . . pick things up. But it wasn't easy. It's a business run by old, bloated, bitter, and impotent men, so they don't like someone half their age and female coming along and proving them wrong, because when you're old, bloated, bitter, and impotent, your expertise is the only thing left."

"It must take years to learn the business."

"Years."

"That's my problem, I've never found the right thing. I've done dozens of jobs, dancer on cruise ships, waitressing, driver, box office, security guard—in a word, anything badly paid or really dreadful, but they've all been jobs that didn't go anywhere. You're so lucky to have an interesting job. But I mustn't witter on, I'm sure you've got things to do. A man to attend to."

"No, at the moment, that's one problem I haven't got."

"Enjoy the peace and quiet while you can, then. One'll blunder along any moment in need of coddling."

Rosa goes to have a bath. Nikki does the dishes as the dishes have never been done before; surfaces are scoured. A promise has been made of a mushroom stew for the next day. Rosa vacates the bathroom, Nikki enters, studying Rosa's legs, swallowing a thought.

Rosa goes for the phone: "Yes, it's genuine, but . . . I don't know how to put this, I'm not sure what sort of genuine it is. I'd like to hang on to it for a bit longer." Silence. "It's difficult to explain." Silence. Listening. "Well, you'll think me crazy, but I have the feeling the bowl is lying."

This will be hard work.

Nikki: Second Day

"You're sure I can stay?" Nikki trills. "I really don't want to be a nuisance."

"No, it's fine. When you live on your own, it's good to have the occasional intrusion."

Departure: Rosa. Staying behind with money left by Rosa, waiting for the washing-machine repairman to call: Nikki.

Nikki has pulled the let-down-by-a-friend-who-owes-her-money scenario; it may well be that there is a friend who owes her money, but there are doubtless many more friends to whom she owes much more money. She sits by the table, calculating her options, when the repairman arrives.

Repairman: well-proportioned, full of himself. No woman or washing machine holds any challenge for him. Tight trousers. Full connoisseuring by Nikki of his privities.

He up-ends and eviscerates the washing machine and swiftly locates the deficient part.

"How much is it going to cost?" inquires Nikki in the tone of voice women use when they know a tapping is on the way but they have to pretend they don't. She is loosely clothed, knowing enough to allow the promise to do the work, rather than simply opening negotiations in the buff. She does tug at her nipples in a way that someone very, very stupid might mistake for her adjusting her top.

"Fine," he says. "But I haven't got much time and you'll still have to pay, if that's what you're thinking about."

Tapping: six minutes, twenty-one seconds. I have never seen a washing machine used like that. Despite the obvious discomfort of the venue, or perhaps because of it, they nuke chryselephantinely. Nikki looks at the repairman with shining respect. He returns the washing machine to its

19

rightful place, gives her a nod of accolade, and walks out slowly without the payment. "You win." Two minutes, fifteen seconds later, there is the distant sound of a car driving into a lamppost.

Nikki redoes her hair and steps out to get the mail. She instinctively casts aside the circulars and the junk. With exquisite care that is a pleasure to watch, she steams open the communications that might contain something stimulating or advantageous.

"Dear Box 59," she reads. "Worry no more, here I am, knight in shining armor in the guise of an outrageously young forty-eight. I work in the film industry and have a knockout lifestyle and electric personality. . . ." She puts down the letter, an unfeigned despair on her features.

"Why? Why are there so many wankers in this world? Where's the factory? I'm not even going to bother sealing up your letter, wanker, I'm not even going to bother ripping you off, just up." She goes to the bathroom, shreds the letter, and flushes it away.

I get to see the unflattering side of people. Not necessarily the worst side, but certainly the side people don't want others to see. Things are done in front of me that wouldn't be done in front of pets; who wants to lose the respect of their hamster? We, the inanimate, are treated with disdain and are subjected to ordeals that few hamsters could face. What the husband doesn't want the wife to see; the wife, the husband; the master, the valet; the valet, the master; the officer, the soldier; the soldier, the officer, we see. Ministers thumb-sucking. Heroes nail-biting. Underwear run for days. Judges pretending to be goats, badly.

Nikki resumes her reading, putting aside one letter with the remark: "Phwwwooarr, I'll give you one." It is the last letter of the collection that incites some major attention.

"I am currently moving, so it would be easier for you to contact me at my work number," she reads and then remarks: "Just the job. Married man looking for a quick florida, I can see you."

She enlists the phone: "Hello, Brian. Box 59 speaking. You can call me Fiona. Loved your letter. Your letter made me . . . come over all funnee. Why don't we meet? No, I mean right now. Okay. Okay. Oh, I could be there in an hour."

She applies a few of Rosa's unguents then leaves. "You better carry lots of cash, Brian."

Return: six hours, forty-eight minutes later, carrying two large shopping bags. She opens up her pouch and counts out bills with satisfaction and then unbags some medicinal-looking containers. She boils some water, and placing some tablets into a piece of paper, folds it up into a small square, then grinds it with a rolling pin; she then withdraws to her room where, leaving the door slightly open presumably so she can hear any approach, she strains the mixture through a series of syringes until she finally injects it into her right foot. Immediately, a look of profound satisfaction takes up residence behind her portholes. Nikki is unequivocally a young lady who needs a vast amount of entertainment.

Return: Rosa. She finds Nikki cheery and domestic. Supper is ready along with the two replies that Nikki deemed suitable for her; one from a retired town planner who wrote that his wife had been encouraging him to take up new interests in retirement and that his buttocks, although sixty-six years old, were round, firm, and no possible source of embarrassment to her and that he would consider his chief merit to be experience. Experience indeed since the dots of his writing reveal him to be eighty-six, but even the gaga want to gogo. It is impressive that Nikki instantly realized that the concept of blackmail would require too much explanation to this gentleman.

The other letter is from a blacksmith in Ipswich who doesn't enclose a photograph of himself but of two wrought-iron fruit bowls, and speaking as the law on bowlwork and beauty (after all, I invented it), I'm far from bowled over: stercoliths. Nikki makes a cup of tea as though she hasn't inspected every comma in Rosa's correspondence. Rosa doesn't seem unduly disappointed by her haul, though she does mutter "Another one" as she tears up the letter and the enclosed order form.

She locks me in for a session. I give her some elephant racing to keep her amused. A natural crowd pleaser. I'm now ready with a string of colorful diversions to prevent her from finding the treasure trove, though I wish she'd hand me over to my prospective owner. The fingering is unsettling.

With a brief good night, Rosa seals herself into her bedroom. In the half-light, Nikki looks into the hallway mirror and lets her lips form the word "Rosa"; then she sticks out her tongue, which extends out and away like a creature that has been hiding in her, further than many would believe credible, wide, weighty, and wet. Inch for inch to the face it lives in it is the nineteenth longest and fifth widest tongue I have ever seen, and mouths are one of my specialties. It oscillates prehensilely, polishes the tip of Nikki's nose, then shoots back.

Nikki: Day Three

Rosa slips out first thing. Her mind is elsewhere, and she leaves the lounge window open a fraction. Nikki, rising an hour later, ponders the open window for a while. Then she gathers up a number of small, eminently portable but valuable items and deposits them in a bag.

Departure Nikki. Return Nikki.

The bag no longer contains the items. While secreting some money in the frame of her rucksack, she phones the police to report a burglary.

The police turn up just before Rosa. Everyone concurs that the culprits entered by the open window.

Rosa is only moderately exasperated by the incident, which could really sink others. Curiously, an air of relief plays around her, even when the policeman gravely informs them that there is little possibility of the stolen items being recovered. His words fall into Rosa's breasts.

"It's all my fault," insists Nikki. "I should have checked the windows before I went out shopping."

"No," says Rosa, "I was the one who left it open."

Nikki cooks her courgette special while Rosa checks her insurance to see whether she can claim on Nikki's behalf for the rings and earrings, given to her by her grandmother, that she says are gone. "I'm really bringing you bad luck," she remorses.

Rosa comes to me for a session. I haven't grassed for a long time, so I give her the story of . . .

The Collector of Jericho

He had grown a passion for ceramics. I entered his collection (as a bull vase) when it was already fully developed with dozens of flasks, bowls, double vases, juglets, ewers as well as such curios as Bes jars, hedgehogs, ducks, a woman suckling, and some misshapen accidents of firing that he thought were works of genius; in my view, the finest pieces were two wavy-handled jars and a ring flask. But collectoring at its best.

Regrettably he discovered parrots. A mania for any and all parrots. There was no such thing, as far as he was concerned, as too many parrots or too much money spent on parrots. If there was money it meant more parrots. I wasn't the only one in the household who felt the world was being unfairly deprived of its parrots. But being a bit lugal, he didn't pay any attention.

After years of this obsession, he acquired a loud blue parrot, a parrot no one had ever heard or seen before. Cost a granary—for it came from beyond the end of the world, two shipwrecks away. This squawking blue pest became the center of his pride, so one morning when he discovered a parrotless perch, he hovered with rage. There was no doubt it had been stolen, since its chain, large enough for a boisterous dog, lay cracked on the ground. Wrathfully, he offered huge rewards for the recovery of the parrot.

In the event, he only had to wait a few days. The parrot was spotted by the Great Gate, playing dice for money; unusually for this sort of mountebank show, the parrot was losing heavily, much to the annoyance of the parrot's backer, an Eblaite.

The Eblaite was brought to judgement and swore by seventeen gods that he had known the parrot since it was an egg, that he had known its parents since they were eggs, that he had seen its grandparents as eggs, and he was a poor showman only coming under the weight of this terrible accusation because he was of humble station and from a distant land, that he had a ghastly toothache and that in Ebla, blue parrots were so numerous they fell out of the trees because there wasn't enough room for them all to perch.

Three Eblaites then entered the court and testified that they had never seen parrots, let alone blue ones, in Ebla; on the other hand, they had seen the accused before, who was known for his sticky fingers and, despite using loaded dice, always losing.

The accused shouted that these three had proved they

weren't Eblaites since they didn't know about the parrots; they were in fact Elamites, notorious for their traditional hatred of the Eblaites, who were only testifying against him because they fancied an impaling.

The tribunal asked him to handle the parrot. It bit him. The collector was then summoned, and the parrot settled on his arm, repeating his name and the name of his wife. The Eblaite invoked twenty-five gods, including all of Jericho's favorites, and two fetishes he had in his pocket to swear that the parrot was his and merely sulking because he had remonstrated with it on its dice technique. He tried to get the parrot to repeat a phrase, any phrase, and attempted to give it a playful stroke. The parrot bit him again, drawing blood.

After being sentenced to lingering death for theft, perjury, and inventing gods without a license, the Eblaite offered to make a full confession in exchange for clemency and to recount six other crimes committed in other cities that he was sure the tribunal would find droll.

"You may have the gift of gab," he cursed the parrot as he was dragged away, "but you're shit at dice. They were right when they said I should have stuck with the monkeys."

The Eblaite, as it turned out, wasn't the only one who cursed the parrot. Not long after the Eblaite's bones had been picked clean, the collector discovered that his best friend was carrying out the repetition that people rarely find repetitive with his wife as the result of graphic imperatives repeated by the parrot, coupling the most intimate parts of his wife's anatomy with his friend's name. If you're snitching you should know what you're doing.

His best friend didn't have quite the lugaling position the collector did, so he ended up having him killed, exposed with the parrot inserted in his bottom. It's the eighth slowest form of death I have encountered (for humans, that is), essentially dying of thirst with massive discomfort. I'm not sure how it ranks for parrots. There was a maharajah who tried to insert one of his irritating courtiers into an elephant's posterior: "You're the biggest turd I've ever met; there's only one place for you." However, the elephant wasn't acquiescent and broke the courtier's neck shaking him out, for which, in all probability, the courtier was grateful.

The collector, to be honest, never really enjoyed anything again—his parrots, us crocks, or his life. Relish banished. *Nisaba zami*, as we used to *dubsar* in Lagash.

Rosa

Rosa is sitting on the ground, overhistoried, pasted by the past. "Phew," she emits eventually and stumbles toward her bedroom.

"Are you all right?" Nikki asks.

"No. Yes. I'm not, but I am. Don't worry. Good night."

Day Four of Nikki

First exiting: Rosa. Second exiting: Nikki, wearing leggings and a leotard under her topcoat, having fired in a partnership of benzedrine and methadone. First reentry: Nikki, five hours, three minutes later, visibly having indulged in vigorous physical exercise. She is accompanied by a hefty, quiffed youth. She identifies some larger, heavier items, which are for the purloining and which he consents to take down to his van.

"What about this flower pot?" he mutters. "Oh, it's cracked," he says chucking me on the floor, breaking me into three pieces. I am richly vilipended by their refusal to consider me marketable. By the meanest of assessments I am worth his van, thrice. He conveys out the microwave, the television, a fine-looking suitcase, Rosa's collection of music, lamps, a bookshelf, the answering machine, plants, the washing machine, and chairs while Nikki gets out of her moist clothes. Reenter the remover, who tries to act as if naked women are an everyday occurrence in his crimes.

"I forgot to ask, sweaty or not?" she asks.

Apparently sweaty's acceptable, but he can't understand why she wants to situate the tapping on the table by the window and not the bed. "People can't see us there." Chryselephantine pleasure for seven minutes, sixteen seconds, culminating in Nikki hanging out the window, barking, and one of the table legs collapsing.

"A pity about that," remarks the remover. "Could have got a few quid for that table." He counts out some bills for Nikki, who watches him drive off before reporting the burglary to the police. Shattered unbeknownst to Nikki, I reassemble unbeknownst to Nikki, carefully re-creating my former cracks.

The same policeman appears. Nikki's physical exertions help give credence to her pretence at being disheartened. "They sometimes come back like this. Was there a set of keys taken last time?" He asks after Rosa. Nikki explains that she won't return till the evening.

Later, Rosa calls. Nikki unleashes a brilliant incoherent-with-distress routine, scarcely managing a complete sentence, bewailing the thefts and claiming that her underwear was interfered with during the action. Rosa has apparently broken down in her car and tells Nikki not to wait with supper for her and takes the time to soothe her specious suffering.

Nikki goes to the cabinet in the bathroom and checks the bottle of aspirin to see how many are in it; you can see she's contemplating pulling the I-can't-go-on ploy, but you have to be certain you don't take too many, that you'll be found punctually and you can see she isn't in the mood for a stomach-pumping. All in all, it's odd that with such guile, a glut of unscruples, and glee in destroying others' lives, she has no more to her name or names than a rucksack full of clothes; she should be running a country somewhere.

After dark, the policeman reappears. "Is your flatmate back?" he asks politely.

"No," says Nikki.

"I should say I'm here off-duty. In a private, nonpolice sort of capacity, if you see what I mean."

"That's a bit cheeky."

"Well, we're only human."

"No, you're not," says Nikki, then grinning. "Come on in and wait for her if you want. An hour." Her stamina is admirable, you can see she's tired, but she still, like a true champion, responds to any challenge. This girl can go. She is, of course, voracious enough just to rip off his breeches, an approach that has only been refused by men to my knowledge twice in the last six thousand years, but she wants to see how his timidity can be dismantled. She flutters her eyelids, evinces admiration that is too much for her face as he recounts the things he has found on the other side of the public's doors; bad acting on a stage might earn you harsh notices, but it nearly always works offstage.

The policeman must have been quite keen on Rosa, because it is in fact fifty-six minutes before he takes the plunge into Nikki's mouth. He is unpackaged and read like a gas meter. He stares down fixedly so he has a chance to believe what is being done to his statuette. After three minutes, eight seconds, she looks him in the eyes and says, "Come." He obliges, one seminal expedition ascending to the ceiling; he is maxed out and offers Nikki some drugs that he takes to schools to lecture on the evils of narcotics; Nikki partakes liberally. He tries to unscrew the jar of pickled beetroot. "I can't understand," he says on the way out, "I've had my cock for twenty-eight years but you can do it so much better."

Rosa turns up. Nikki offers her the remaining chair. You have to admire her resilience in the face of misfortune, quite blighting. Something else is keeping her from expending time in gnashing of teeth. She is lonely; it is a faint smell, too elusive for a human nose, but I can detect it. Worn, forlooooooorn, but not by what has happened in the flat.

She comes to me. Her fingers take my sides; she is, I sense, not keen to take out information, but desirous of coming in. I choose for her. . . .

My Favorite Shipwreck

The voyage to Byblos: when Troy still had joy. The sailing had been a mistake. It was dark even for a winter night, a storm. Various needs, greeds, and idiocies had launched the ship.

There were two young people on the ship: the Mop (I call him such because of his long thick hair) and the painter's daughter, whose beauty would have enthralled any city let alone a small boat.

The Mop was bursting with youth and made his money by stunt swimming, butterflying from island to island, racing against galleys, doing aquatic tricks. It was a small boat, and I can't have been the only one to have thought how wonderfully they would have linked.

The painter's daughter was friendly and joked with the sailors, was nice to the emaciated idea-merchant who spent

29

most of his time in his thought plantation, asked about the knots, and chatted with everyone except the Mop, who couldn't manage to get his mouth to work. He would sneak up to her with his eyes, but he was so keen on getting in right that he would do nothing wrong. Two days out and he still hadn't addressed a word to her—quite an achievement on such a small boat; he sat under a pile of rags as if this were something important and needful for him, while everyone else discussed the weather, how to prepare tuna, the price of grain, and the earrings of Caphtor.

The truly frightening weather was sudden, but not sudden enough for the occupants not to have time to think about it. The skipper started to cry. There was talk of which gods to go for. The all-over look was all over. Everyone there in that cold, dark valley of waves would have murdered their family to escape; death comes in more cuddly forms.

The sea frolicked on the deck and fondled the ankles of the skipper and the helmsman, who were busy employing their hands to throttle each other. One of the crew grabbed a goatskin, as much use in that storm as going into a forest fire with a glass of water.

"Come on, the boat's going to try and drink the sea," he shouted, offering another goatskin to the idea-merchant now seated in the sea.

"Nothing happens," the idea-merchant riposted.

"The ship's going to be shafted by the deep in fifty-seven positions."

"That's your interpretation, not mine."

"We're sinking."

"Why must you look at things that way? It won't do you any good."

The painter's daughter casts off her bracelets, reaches for her earrings—gold with dolphin terminals—then, thinking those who might find her body might treat it better if she carries funeral costs, leaves them and looks impassively at the sea of icy ink. The moon couldn't bear to watch. The water follows her robe up her body as she takes it off. Then a hand stretches out to her.

"Wait. Let's go together," says the Mop.

They held hands and they managed a few swirling steps before the ship bade farewell to their feet. Having seen two million four hundred thousand nine hundred and twenty-seven couples hold hands, I have never seen such a touching touch.

I pendulumed down to the quiet of the sea bed, letting out oooooos of air fleeing back to the turbulence of the surface, mixing with the other oooooos of the talker, who was fitting into those little bubbles bits of the exclamation: "Nothing happens." Certainty pays all bills.

(Are you wondering, Rosa, what happened to the Mop and the painter's daughter? Would you like to know what happened to them? So would I. I have looked for traces of them in every face I see.)

Lullabied, Rosa sleeps the sleep of those of us who've known the deep.

Though she pulled out before the thirty years of mackerel, sea lizards, and turbots. Let's not get started on the turbots. There's no one here who knows more about turbot than me. A million turbots aren't as turboted up as me. Let's not even mention them. Turbot city. The turbot dark age. The turbots more than anything else were behind my return to the surface. The only good turbot is one that's working its way down a digestive tract. You try and lurk in the murk, but you get no peace. However, the conger eel with the earring was worth meeting. To date I have only encountered one conger eel with an earring. Silver it was. Wonderful workmanship.

Nikki: Day Five

Rosa continues to depart betimes. She produces a catalogue from her bag and leaves it on the table on her way out. I wish she hadn't. It boasts a rich reproduction of a vase with a Gorgon's head on it. A copy of a copy of a copy of a copy. Maybe a copy of a copy of a copy of a copy of a copy. One of the Athenian ones. Not that that will save it. I go for them as far as a copy of a copy of a copy of a copy of a copy of a copy.

Nikki picks up the catalogue and, to my intense annoyance, looks with favor on the cover vase. Her approbation unfortunately reminds me of . . .

The Endless Hatred (That Never Ends)

It was in the workshop. "Someone must have done it," said the master. "Or someone must have brought it in. Vases don't just stroll in because they like the look of the workshop."

"It's not possible. No one went in or out," insisted the apprentices, who had slept there throughout that hot Corinthian night.

"Well, what's it doing here?" snapped the master, cuffing him. "Some rich ordure will come in and claim it his. We are being aligned with misfortune. We will be punished as thieves. Go and tell everybody in the other places that we've found a vase."

"Why's the gaffer in such a foul mood?" asked one apprentice.

"Rotten teeth," the other replied.

They didn't notice that the old water pitcher was gone. I was now resplendent as a double-handled amphora with a Gorgon's face. I fancied a change of scenery, and there's nothing like getting flash for getting the cash. Everyone came to have a look at me, and there were suitable gasps of amazement at the rendering and the color.

Naturally, everyone in the workshop was determined to have a go at imitating me; once you know it can be done, it's easier. They all tried, but it was the youngest apprentice who went audaciously with the glaze who did best, although his Gorgon was feeble.

But when it came out of the kiln, they all gathered around and clapped, much more than was deserved, I thought. Then the competition came in, the dimpled potter in the lead, and instead of denigrating the ware and highlighting any flaw and ignoring any flair, they shook their heads in disbelief.

"The vase you found, that was nice, but this, I've never seen anything like this. It's alive. You know, in the evenings I love to come and belittle your wares, and I've spent twenty years doing that, making the most disparaging remarks about your general appearance, the company you keep, and your family; but I can't do that now. This is a glory that we all benefit from." The other potters stood around, murmuring in agreement. "No one in our lifetimes will produce finer work." The apprentice was unable to stand, he was so overwhelmed with praise, and I was getting a bit tetchy. "The lines on the vase you discovered are clumsy and amateurish," said the Dimple, "whereas on this they have the strength of life."

Then the moneybags who hadn't gone to the new-look games at Olympia arrived and oofed all over them. The whole workshop, not to mention the surrounding workshops, went wild knocking out Gorgons. They were ropey Gorgons, but the purchasers turned up and forked out prices that had never been invented before. I wasn't sold. It would be nice to note here that the workshop master held on to me out of a sense of gratitude, but this wasn't the case. Every day he tried to unload me. "I don't want a cheap copy" was one of the more polite refusals, even when I was being offered at a derisory price.

I declared war. Having invented beauty and the enslavement of light, I don't much care for my work to be disparaged. It was my prompting that took memory out of the mind and onto surfaces, made the private public. Cadmus has his lines, I have mine. I showed them how to make the beauty traps, and the third-rate should be punished.

Here's the score of crushed Gorgons: 1,648.

Nikki Resumed

Nikki casts aside the catalogue.

Finally, ineluctably, it's my turn to be stolen. Insultingly, Nikki holds me and says, "Bet it won't be worth carrying this to the shop." This is the three thousand two hundred and ninth time I have been stolen, not to mention the one hundred and two occasions I have been borrowed in goodish faith without being returned.

Despite having just perused an auction catalogue, Nikki has no thought of considering me as an antique. That's the problem with art, indeed, many other things; you have to fit in with the expectations. Pity the priceless things that have been dumped in the trash, the treasures that have been melted down, the master thoughts that have ended up wiping the arses of the ignorant.

I am stuck in a carrier bag with a food mixer, a small lamp, a red alarm clock, and a garish ashtray. Nikki has clearly decided to move on from Rosa's and to milk the last few coins from the property. Rosa left, saying she'd be away for two days.

Nikki carries us down a high street where we pass a black

couple copulating in a doorway next to a bus stop; the man shrieks at the people in the queue: "What are you looking at?"

We enter a junk shop and Nikki presents us to the proprietor, who regards us with contempt so undisguised it might as well have been on a trampoline, not just because he is building up to making an insulting offer, but because like nearly everyone who works in the secondhand trade, he works in it because he revels in inflicting cruelty on others, especially the desperate or the needy.

Nikki has approached with a pathetic, tear-stained face and, not to leave pity to fight the battle on its own, her cleavage more open than the cool weather would invite. The Tatman's pulse immediately races, not at the sight of her sternum, but at the prospect of distress.

He holds the objects one by one, reluctantly, as if they had been licked by bad-breathed lepers.

"I wouldn't sell that if it weren't for my son's needing an operation. My mother gave it to me just before she died," says Nikki as I am pawed. "I think it's an antique."

Respiration increases; he rocks on his feet with excitement. His member shuffles in its fabric silo.

"I think it isn't."

Biting the inside of her mouth to get a good watering in her eye, Nikki says, "It must be worth something."

I am held gingerly between pollex and finger as if I were a dried cowpat.

"Yeah. It's worth something. It's worth fuck-all. There isn't much call for really ugly flower pots. Can't remember the last time I had someone in the shop saying I want a really rough flower pot."

It's hard to imagine anyone coming into the shop even if they wanted to buy something. The air is moldy, and even

with the detraction of rot, the items are the worst sort of rubbish, unloved, unlovable artifacts, most abandonable trap-
pings; anything with any value would shoot out of here like a
bubble of air going toward the surface to rejoin its friends. I
make a note to do him a major disservice should I get the
chance. He lines us objects up on the counter, adjusting us
slightly here and there to get what he considers a straight
line. The food mixer is new.

"Short of some cash, eh darling?" He wants to hear it. She
trots out the son-in-hospital-without-toys patter. His heart
goes to maximum.

"A pound." He almost swoons as he sees the look worth a
book on Nikki's face. He construes it as pain, but it is, truthfully, anger. It's not an offensive offer, it's not an offer at all;
it's offering offense, it's someone pissing on your shoes and
thinking it hilarious. Which is unwise, since whatever else
Nikki is, undangerous she is not. I wonder if she will go for
the knife carried expertly in her boot and help herself to the
till. The Tatman has no fight, only malice in him.

She gathers us up and gets as far as the door. Tatman,
sensing that the fun is over and that he's not going to get her
to whimper and blub, coughs up a tenner because she has
such beautiful eyes; Nikki doesn't see this as worth the effort
of walking to the shop, but she has had enough of this final
attempt at cashing in on Rosa.

I am placed next to a velvet giraffe carrying almost as
much life as a real giraffe, a helter-skelter of mechanical penguins that don't work, and a ceramic badger wearing cricket
flannels. This is a unique artifact. It cannot have been owned
by anyone. It is unownable, it is constantly in search of
appreciation, appreciation it will not get. To look on it is to
despair. It is a pariah, passed from hand to hand, though
oddly enough not to a bin. Made to be rejected. It will have

been left here, not bought. The Tatman hasn't changed his underwear for three days.

The Mummy That Cried for Earth

The velvet giraffe reminds me of the mummy I was entombed with. When the grave robbers broke in, I have to say I was grateful; we all like a break, but a thousand years is enough. The mummy was no one you'd care to know about; a moderately successful oil supervisor who managed to die of natural causes, having reproduced and earned enough for me and other objects to be sealed up with him.

It was a few owners later that I met up again with the supervisor. When I was lifted from the tomb, they weren't interested in the mummies. It was through Wondernose (One Hundred and Sixteen), who was one of the wiliest grave robbers, that I was reunited decades later with my tombmate. To be accurate, he wasn't a grave robber, he was a grave-robber robber. He didn't believe in laboring away digging or wandering thorough labyrinthine passages, sneaking through cracks or bringing down the wrath of long-gone but maybe not dead gods. He would wait till some other malfeasants had looted a site and were almost back at the city when he would appear and help himself.

"Where's my reward?" the tipper-offer asked when I was snatched from the snatchers. "You have it already," Wondernose said. "Think about it, you're still breathing." Wondernose would then return home, wary lest anyone decided to try and become a grave-robber-robber robber.

He didn't get much trouble over his nose. Firstly, because while people are prepared to die for an idea, they're not, in my observation, keen to die for a joke. Besides which, his nose was of such magnitude that it was too obvious to make a joke about it. Exaggeration can make an ordinary thing funny, but overexaggeration brings it back to the unfunny. It was rather like saying the sun's shining today and expecting people to laugh. He had a nose rest for it and would store small fruits in it.

Money was Wondernose's torment. He did good business, but at night he would find sleep elusive; what needled him was the thought that others would be making more. If he sold a blue hippopotamus to a merchant in Alexandria for five, he would, with the sight of night, see the merchant smirking, selling it again for fifty. Then he could see someone across the waters selling it for a hundred and guffawing. Farther on in the icy wastes, someone selling it for five hundred, and finally, in the farthest north, someone selling it for a thousand and coiled up in pain from extreme mirth. "They're laughing at me."

It simmered for a long time. "Five," a merchant would say. "Ten," Wondernose would respond. "Seven then," the merchant would cede reluctantly. "Twenty," Wondernose would retort.

"I said seven," said the merchant.

"Thirty," said Wondernose.

"Look, I need good luck to find someone to sell it to for ten. I've had these blue hippopotamuses for over a year."

"Forty," says Wondernose, getting angry. The merchant had to call on several members of his family, including his wife and two of his daughters, in order to eject Wondernose, who was snarling: "You think you're funny, don't you?" His old buyers would have nothing more to do with him since they found it was impossible to contract a price with him and throwing him out disrupted the cooking of the evening meal.

Wondernose went to Tyre. He asked for merchants who dealt in these things. Having introduced himself to the first one, he punched him in the stomach and then started kicking him around the floor: "So you think I'm funny, do you? Thought you could have a laugh at my expense. A plague on your money."

He hadn't even managed to show the second merchant a blue hippopotamus before he decided to bang his head vigorously on a charming mahogany table, remarking, "Why aren't you laughing now? Aren't I funny anymore?" As soon as he saw the third merchant, he swung for him, shouting, "Fuck your money, fuck your money." Word spread.

Because of this and because he had long harbored the ambition of stopping the man in the frozen north from laughing, he took passage on a ship to Constantinople with his favorite goods. He had with him the mummy, since this was the time when Europeans were amusing themselves at their tea parties by unwrapping mummies, and he thought he would clean up with this cargo. He didn't notice that the crew were sniggering the whole journey because they knew he had been charged five times the normal rate, about a pyramid's worth of grave robbing.

In Constantinople, he tried a number of merchants who spoke Arabic; they offered him the same prices he had scorned in Alexandria. He went farther on to Venice, where they offered him even less. He sold some things to get money to go farther, but he received adulterated coin, and he was arrested when he tried to use it. Then most of his stock disappeared in an earthquake, reclaimed in a snap by the ground.

With the bribes to get out of prison, a fee for a letter composed in Latin by a scribe—which Wondernose believed described him as a man of high estate and import, but actually labelled him a dangerous ruffian who should be cudgeled on sight (scribe joke)—Wondernose had nothing left but me, a blue hippopotamus in his left pocket, and the mummy. Nevertheless, he struggled on northward, with no shoes and a severe toothache, adamant that the great sale was nigh.

Finally, we reach Helsinki. We are ushered into the chamber of a lawyer, a collector of curios. He has been sent here in the snow because the collector is famous for purchasing any exotic rubbish, so as soon as Wondernose appeared in the vicinity, he was pointed in the right direction.

As we proceed in, Wondernose knows he is in the presence, finally, of the Great Sniggerer. Wondernose doesn't pay much attention to the two-bodied lamb, the rat kings, assorted terata, mammoth's tusks, and other poorly arranged rarities. Wondernose forgets about the months of hardship he had endured, the three toes he has lost from frostbite, as he unveils me and the mummy. You lash yourself to your idea and you sink or you swim.

There is one hunger nearly as great as the need for sleep, food, or water but because its pangs are not so acute or debilitating as physical needs, its power is sometimes overlooked: The mind needs rules. Rules are the true rulers. And one set is only thrown aside when another is ready. The sun rises, the sun sets. You give your gods nidor, they give you health. Trade: You go to the wish shop and buy. One tidal wave less, please. One bumper crop more. As a child puts everything in its mouth, so man puts everything in rules. If your favorite pig dies, there must be a reason. Nothing is more frightening than no rules; people will cherish the worst rules as long as they can avoid the prospect of a sky that spits in their face for no reason. The sensation that nobody wants to feel: Fortune is off the leash.

That's my nickname for all of them: the rule makers. No matter where, no matter how they differ, they make rules. Don't eat this. Don't eat that. It's improper to wear more than six earrings at once. Don't kiss on a first date. If an ubarum, a naptarum, or a mudum wants to sell his beer, the sabitum shall sell the beer for him. Balance the legislature, the executive, and the judiciary. Luck, the fuck. The propagation of rules is abetted by the prosperous flaunting of their rules as if they had something to do with their success. Hence also the allure of secrecy: deluxe rules under the counter.

The lawyer (Bloodsuckerissimus the Five Thousand Four Hundred and Thirty-Second) picks at the mummy. The former oil supervisor is not looking good, having been left out in the rain, dropped in mud, with a fungus of a stimulating green hue sprouting on his shoulders.

"I've got two already," says Bloodsuckerissimus. "I bought them last year. Though the fungus is very tempting. As for the blue hippopotamus . . ." He gestures to a shelf where there are three lesser but indisputable blue hippopotamuses.

Wondernose is standing there, wishing he understood a word of what is being said. However, when the unmistakable international gesture of noooooo-take-your-goods-elsewhere-the-door-is-over-there is made, he is demolished, the last masonry of the soul crumbles.

At this point, in comes an excited peasant, burrowing into the carpet with his groveling. "Your illustriousnessing, I have found a marvel beyond belief." He unpacks a huge, frozen iguana. "A dragon, your illustriousingness, a young dragon." Bloodsuckerissimus is unimpressed. He goes to a book, opens to a page with an illustration of an iguana, and shows it to the peasant.

"What's this?" the lawyer demands.

"A dragon, your illustriousingness."

"No, it's not. Let me introduce you to the letters i, g, u, a, n, and I'm sure you remember our old friend a. The iguana is a reptile from the distant Americas."

"But what would such a creature be doing here? This one has no wings."

"I'm sure the iguana's last thoughts, on an iguana sort of basis, would have been precisely that. I surmise if you look hard enough, you'll find a drunken sailor wailing for his lost pet. It's good of you to show me this, but I already have two larger specimens."

The peasant looks at his dreams spilled on the ground. Wondernose's patience snaps. He goes for the frozen iguana and attempts to clobber Bloodsuckerissimus, but his target is not unfamiliar with people wanting to inflict grave physical injury on him. He dodges and takes up the femur of the former supervisor to fend off his assailant. They flail around, exhibits are dented or cracked, the peasant has his four remaining teeth sunk into Wondernose's calf in a new project of ingratiation. Servants appear, and still using the frigid weapon, Wondernose fights his way out, rushing away into the Great White.

Outcomes: Wondernose was discovered in the spring, when he thawed and fell out of a tree he had taken shelter in. Bloodsuckerissimus took a death mask so people would believe him when he talked about the nose.

Myself as blue hippopotamus: taken into the collection, discreetly, by lawyer.

Mummy: No one really wanted it. Unearthed, passed from robber to robber, snubbed by merchant after merchant, it had traveled thousands of miles, only to be shunted back into the ground. Posthumous failure. Local priest heard about it, took it from authorities, decided to christen it and bury it. He had a thing about converting heathens and had welcomed the opportunity on the doorstep.

Frozen iguana: vanished as bizarrely as it had appeared. A strand that appears often, the unbelievable. The unbelievable occurs a lot. Granted, it isn't always as exotic or as far-fetched as an Egyptian grave robber clubbing a Finnish mouthpiece with an icy saurian, but it is no less unbelievable for being boring or dreary or bereft of frozen iguanas. The unbelievable doesn't just come in frozen-iguana flavor, it comes in never-loved-furniture flavor too, never-left-home flavor, still-not-met-anyone-interesting flavor, can't-get-a-job flavor. But finally, the unbelievable is the hallmark of the believable.

Tatman's

The Tatman watches Nikki leave, cheered that he had a chance to see a beauty in distress (after all, misfortune is the uniform of the ugly), disappointed he couldn't wring more tears out of her. That Nikki jettisoned the semblance of anguish before the cash hit her palm doesn't register. Stupidity pays generously.

I consider doing some shaping. There are very few things as scary as turning around and finding an eight-foot-high amphora behind you when there wasn't one before, especially when that amphora is making faces at you. Most people foul themselves and find it very hard to trust reality and relax after that. Once every three hundred years or so, I treat myself.

Even for me, this is a low point in my ceramicking; condemned, it seems, to catch grimy drops weaseling their way through the ceiling from some filthy source above. Fifteen molds are on the premises. The bacteria, I won't bother about. Before I can summon up the three hundred and nineteen situations worse than this one, a woman walks into the shop.

Those without my honed capabilities might not have spotted at the first look that she is a woman.

43

She is large. She is not the largest woman I have ever seen, but she comes in at number six, only five pounds behind number five. Three hundred and thirty-two to five pounds, that's some five sleeping Sumerian ducks (the two-talent ones oooooobviously) or nearly three thousand breathless voles (measurements, like rules, are also important, because without them you can't have the pleasure of cheating—the vole-ridden tribe that took them as a standard was soon spending all its time fattening them up or just filling them with sand; it was one of those unioccurring ideas that never caught on, but it is, nevertheless, my favorite avoirdupois).

Six-four. A lot of anyone's cubits. She is so bulky that the building suddenly looks flimsy, and you could imagine her walking through the wall as easily as the door. Her hair is white and cropped to no more than the breadth of a finger (unless you have extremely thick fingers). She wears a pair of earrings betokening a passerby struggling to get into a burning building to save trapped children.

A lot of light is blocked from getting into the shop.

"The woman who just came in. I want everything she sold you."

She is wearing a white leather jacket; on the back of the jacket, fastened in an unskilled manner, are two wings. They are the wings, I note, of a condor, the other condory bits disposed of, painted white, again not particularly skillfully.

Tatman is surprised by such huge custom from such a huge customer with such huge wings, but not that much; we are indubitably in a neighborhood where personal expression is welcomed. Making money is not his primary aim, so he needs a few moments to pump up the price to a nearly indefensible level. He strokes the items in front of him with instantaneous respect, he fits in his selling voice, but unfortunately he has to push it, he has to go for the supplement of outrage to take home with him that evening so he doesn't stop when he gets to me, but he tries to work in the penguins, the giraffe, and the ceramic badger as well.

"Two hundred quid."

"Do you want me to hit you?" she asks with what I can only describe as extreme courtesy and warmth. Her delivery is so at odds with the message that Tatman almost misses it: that this is a woman so powerful she could pull his limbs off one by one, like petals off a flower.

He drops the assorted animals hastily, since we are also in a neighborhood where people have been excessively injured for lesser trespasses, but she pays the one hundred pounds he asks for the original package without a murmur. We depart.

Outside, a black youth is riding his bike on the pavement; he rides up to my new carrier, clearly expecting her to get out of his way. He wears a Walkman and, despite it being an overcast November afternoon, sunglasses. He screws up his eyes behind the glasses and is thinking about saying something. My carrier looks seraphic. He lazily detours his bike and rolls ten feet before starting to swear. A man in a wheelchair is loading a child's bike into the trailer attached to his wheelchair; there are thirty-two ways to load a child's bike into your trailer (of that size); this is one of the three ways of loading a child's bike that doesn't belong to you. A man is out buying a pair of black shoes for his wife, who has just died. The average pulse rate on the street is seventy-nine. The two most common thoughts among the passersby, sixty in number: Four people are thinking about potatoes, two about what they'd like to do to the girl in the leopard-skin coat. Seventy-four motor vehicles go past.

We get into a van, which shrinks once my carrier is in. We start off and it is soon apparent that we are heading back to Rosa's. Parked around the corner, my carrier picks up a mobile phone and punches a number. Nikki answers. My carrier then hangs up, ponders, starts up the van, and we go off for another fifteen minutes. We arrive at a gym, the sort of place where the exercising isn't to burn off fat or to shape women's buttocks; this is for the shaping of violence. Boxers pound bags not to sweat but to improve the damage they are going to do. There are improbably large men whose faces have almost disappeared in their muscles, though they don't seem so large next to my carrier. Heads turn as the carrier moves along, the only woman in the place.

"Hello, Lump," says one who knows her. Some others who don't, laugh. Someone has left a minute weight on a bar; Lump tries Rosa's number again, and on discovering that Nikki is still there, she grasps the weight, which she is capable of picking up, along with the person who had been using it, and throwing both into the middle of next week; and she begins to curl it in a blatantly feeble and ungainly manner.

Sure enough, some of the muscle stokers nearby start guffawing at this; there's not much point in having spent most of your life lifting bits of metal and breathing in others' armpits if you can't have a laugh at a floor-breakingly fat woman who doesn't have the wherewithal to lift a bar properly and who is wearing a white leather jacket with mangy white wings on. A group of three inflatables who wouldn't have enough personality between themselves to be a pencil take a break to heap derision on her. I wonder if she is doing this to provoke a fight, since her actions are obviously intended to gather attention and invite scorn.

"You'll never get rid of the flab like that, love," one opines, which is unfair since very little of her body weight is fat; her forearm is the largest in the joint. I sense one or two of the other exercisers in the background are grinning, not because of Lump but because of what is going to happen.

The taunter has a perforation mark tattooed around his neck and the words CUT HERE; he reeks of the weight room in jails. He probably didn't mind jail because he could lift weights, and being in jail prevented him from having opportunities to bugger up his life further. He is a born dickhead, who started off huge and who sweats harder to be a bigger one every day. He doesn't realize he comes from a factory that was in full swing before the Ice Age.

"You'll never get to heaven. Is that why you're here, you trying to float up?" They're rolling. Lump takes this ribbing cherubically for a while.

"Strength's nothing to do with muscles," she says innocently as a nine-year-old schoolgirl. They love it; they haven't seen a loony this fruity for years. "Strength comes from the soul," she says. They're almost incontinent.

"How about a bet?" she proposes. This is the point where anyone with a speck of intelligence knocking about in their skull would take the laughter and leave. But they don't see they're being set up.

"I've got a hundred quid that says I'm tougher than any of you," she says.

"Oh, yeah?" says Perforation.

"Yes," she says, producing two cigarette lighters—one blue, one red—from her pocket along with the cash. Perforation rushes around to rustle up the money. "Choose your lighter," she says. He holds the blue lighter in his right hand, above which is Lump's palm, and in Lump's right hand is the red lighter, above which is his left palm. The flames snake out.

Perforation's discomfort emerges instantly. He is the kind

of person who would rather die than look unhard, but he doesn't get the chance to die, merely to feel excruciating pain. After ten seconds he is trembling with agony and moves his hand up for a moment, then with tears in his eyes, he forces it down. Lump's hand remains motionless, her face beatific. After seventeen seconds, Perforation folds, crying like a child. Smaller, less violent people in the gym are pressed for money by Perforation's black friend, convinced he can do better. Switching lighters, he doesn't.

"It's a con," says Perforation, snatching the blue lighter, igniting it and burning himself again. "You're not getting the money," he says. She looks him sweetly in the eyes while she grabs his family jewels, pulls, squeezes, and twists. She is used to doing this—her smiling, her unwavering look, the way she was standing, weren't accidental, she was getting ready. He has that moment of shock men do when they know about the pain that's left the station and try, as always unsuccessfully, to brace themselves. He deflates.

"I have a word for you," she says. "*Aposematic. A-p-o-s-e-m-a-t-i-c.* Should I write that down for you? The person who you're laughing at might not be fatter but stronger."

Recashed, we drive back to Rosa's. The van is parked, and my carrier gets out and crosses the road, carrying a set of keys. I observe her checking that no one is at home and then fiddling with the door, suggesting to me that she is attempting to break in.

While she is tinkering with Rosa's door, a gentleman I have not encountered before tries the door of the van, gaining entry in parallel with Lump, whom I now suspect will be one of my former carriers. We're off again.

We don't drive far. The stop is a backstreet garage where the gentlemen empties the van of its contents. He moves with the assurance of the demented. Indubitably, if you can find the right sort of obsessive to obsess in the way you want, they're the best employees in the world: no tea breaks, no fatigue, no phone calls, no distractions.

He vacuums the interior of the van meticulously, washes and then waxes the exterior, changes the oil, puts in a new pine tree, shampoos the furry dice, empties the ashtrays of hard-dying smut, polishes the van's tool kit, rearranges the glove compartment, and in the end, after some reflection, resprays the entire van. I get a robust scouring. Five hours later, the van is returned to where it was taken from with a note on the front seat, a copy of the New Testament, and a can of cleaning foam.

The note: *Cleanliness is next to Godliness. A clean vehicle is a vehicle that will surely put you on the highway to salvation. A righteous dashboard is dear to the Lord, lets your vehicle's color brighten your soul. Suggested donation: £100.* It's tricky how to log this one. I opt for borrowed but returned.

My huge carrier lumbers up ten minutes later; Lump has obviously been keeping an eye on the street from a pub and reclaims her van with tranquility. She pockets the card. We get into the flat. She looks around as if she's trying to figure out where the objects belong, but she gives up on that and places us all on the ailing table. She leaves quietly.

Nikki turns up late, evidently having postponed her flight from Rosa's. She is accompanied by a large gentleman who indisputably has a very specific role in the evening's proceedings: to stretch and pummel various parts of her body.

They don't get past the hallway. The man is slight but round-muscled and grunts with a Lyonnais accent; his penis is long and curved. Of the six hundred and eleven types, it is number four hundred and five, the sort that can take your eye out, the scimitar. In addition, his manhood has several pieces of metal jutting out. It resembles a springboard through which several nails have been driven. Nikki makes a sound identical to a Vietnamese pot-bellied pig. They nuke, Nikki bringing into play a cucumber, the vegetable used more than any other for this service (though I did perceive an unforeseen craze for cardoons in the eighteenth century which no one else has commented on), and a wise choice, since a firm cucumber can provide all the grist needed without the risk of permanent residence, a status other tempting objects might aspire to.

She removes the cucumber. "I'll fix us something to eat."

So chryselephantine was the affair that Metaldick is deverbed and debrained for a few minutes. "You're not using that, are you?" he pants on all fours.

"You'll never know the difference. Florida, then a healthy, light meal."

As she moves to the kitchen, Nikki sees us, the much-traveled items on the table. She is stumped, but only for a moment. She checks mentally that she did take us away. She laughs. It is a laugh that suggests she had no idea that Lump is behind the retrieval. She clearly likes mystery as much as being wobbled. Not a girl easily bowed or cowed or in a rush for explanations.

No return for Rosa. As usual, the next morning Nikki needles up and goes off for her exercise, pondering whether to give us another sale.

Next, one hour twenty minutes after Nikki's departure: an authentic, or classic, burglary. The window shatters clankily in the front room, and in comes a long pair of secateurs on telescoped handles used for trimming monstrous hedges. They probe around, but at the moment, after Nikki's predations, there's not much going. With impressive dexterity, the secateurs latch onto an almost empty bottle of whiskey and it is hoisted out of the room. A dry-looking loaf is snatched. Finally, I am grasped and removed.

Outside, the bearded man in a wheelchair looks at me in disgust and annoyance, unaware that if he were ground into mincemeat and sold as the finest dog food and his wheelchair reconditioned and marketed, I would still be worth a thousand times more than that total. One expects a modicum of fervor in one's thieves.

With crime there are two main approaches: stealth or the big brass neck. Unflustered, the Beard (Thirty-Three Thousand and Forty-Nine) rummages in his trailer and produces a whopping, heavy-duty fishing rod which he assembles and then deftly utilizes to hook Nikki's ramshackle radio-cassette player (which had miraculously escaped the earlier clear-outs).

The Beard is unhurried but an emitter of constant obscenity. He checks some papers, which prove to be unprofitable, and then having packed things away in the little trailer behind his chair, far from making any effort to remove himself and us goods from the vicinity, he maneuvers his backside over the edge of the chair and has a leisurely defecation.

Then we're off. First to a newsstand, where he steals a newspaper, then lunch in a nearby café where the Beard pulls up in the center of an aisle so it is completely blocked instead of positioning his train to the side of an empty table and thus allowing others passage. He orders his meal by shouting his desire as loudly and as frequently as his lungs will allow: "Fry-up! Fry-up!" The owner is manifestly familiar with him; his expression carries a number of messages, that he has decided the smoothest option is to serve him and get rid of him, and a regret that civilization has not yet degenerated to the point where he could just stave the Beard's head in with a golf club. The owner has just received a postcard from his brother, explaining how nice it is to run a café in Shropshire.

The Beard shortchanges the owner who notes that he is twenty pence under. "Twenty pence! Twenty pence! Is that so important to you?" He only has to shout this twice before the owner beats a retreat.

Loud eating: a talent the Beard has in trumps. He is truly on the payroll of digustingness. The only part of the newspaper that holds his interest is the obituaries. He reads them aloud with the same relish as he consumes his food and at the same time:

"Yes, yes, die, Eric Allaby, fifty-six, explainer of quantum physics, leaving two sons. Die, die, Auriol Travis, lecturer in Middle Eastern studies, survived by wife and daughter. Die, Air Commodore, eighty-one!" His enthusiasm is roughly the same for all the departed.

As he works his way through the page, Nikki strolls in and looks over the chalked-up menu on the blackboard. From where I am I can see, a hundred yards down the road, the van and its white-haired driver. As she ponders her choice, Nikki spots me and her sonic slave in the trailer. Discreetly, she establishes recognition of her property and leaves.

A couple comes in. The woman in formless clothes to complement her formless body. The man in his forties, with hair that might be described as a haystack in disarray, if a haystack can exist with only twenty pieces of hay. They order tea, but when the waitress brings it in, Hayless opens fire with:

"What's this?"

"Your tea."

Hayless looks around as if he is expecting everyone else to

tisk-tisk in amazement at the outrage that is being perpetrated on him.

"This is not a cup of tea. Please take it away at once."

The waitress is naturally of a high order of politeness and wants to work hard for little money; she is from a poor country. She wants to know what is wrong.

"How can I have a proper cup of tea like that? It should be in a pot." The tea bag floats in the mug.

"I'm sorry," says the waitress, "we normally serve tea like that."

"I don't much care for your attitude," snorts Hayless. The waitress is apologetic, not seeing yet that the problem is not with the tea but with Hayless. She offers to take it away and find a pot.

"No. No. No. Bring me a coffee. You obviously have no idea what a cup of tea is. This is England, you know. It's so basic."

He is almost loud enough to rival the Beard. The waitress rushes back with a coffee.

"No. No. No. It's one insult after the other," says Hayless. "This is not a cup of coffee. I shall have to speak to the management about this." One or two of the other diners look over, log him as a pauseless dickhead. Indeed, waitress tormenting is one of the most despicable crimes; it is usually committed in the more expensive restaurants, but here Hayless is getting it for under a pound. He has obviously not had the fantastic success he feels he deserves and here he has a chance to be listened to and to be unpleasant to someone who has to give smile for his bile. He is, from the way he dresses, concerned about the third world, his pursuits are the extinction of problems, the abolition of suffering. He will write long letters which will never be published in newspapers (unless they have contemptibly small circulations) about the injustice of the world. Even a lugal is better than this feeble jackal, because a lugal tramples everyone, not just the weak or the restrained. His companion is impassive throughout this.

Prognostication: She is inert, without quality qualities and wouldn't cause much excitement among men returned from six years in solitary confinement. Hayless is probably useless in every sense except one: He exists, he is a bed warmer and embarrassment in the odd café is better than loneliness.

Odd that the waitress bothers to work, when down at the underground station, paunchy beggars can pull in a few hours what she gets all day, and they get to insult people. The owner wonders why he isn't in Shropshire, the girl with *The Stage* wonders why she isn't in the Royal Ballet, the mechanic with the greasy hand-rolled cigarette wonders about doing it doggy-style with the tubby cook, but she has given up on romance.

A Nikki reentry five minutes later, when she slips, unobserved by the Beard, another item—a pair of earrings—into the trailer, then a Nikki reexit. The van observes.

Obituary-sniggering goes on for another nine minutes, fifty-three seconds, then we roll out onto the road. Two hundred and fifty-three feet from the café, a police car draws level with us. Well before it's certain that we're the object of their awareness, the Beard reaches for the gas; if he had jettisoned the trailer, he might have given them the slip, since his sturdy arms give tremendous thrust, but he is apprehended.

The arresting officer doesn't have an easy time. The Beard doesn't waste time inquiring about the charge. He yells for help with astonishing volume. "Beat me! Go on, hit me! I'm a cripple! I'm unemployed! I deserve it! Hate me! Witness it. Witness it!" He launches himself out of the chair like a diver, arm thrown back, intent on hitting the pavement, but the policeman breaks his fall. The policeman's right boot is head-butted. He and his colleague land the Beard like a thrashing giant salmon and bundle him into the back of the car.

Cop shop: Having gone as quiet and as malleable as a sullen sack of potatoes, the Beard gets the police off guard and geniusly slams his forehead onto the edge of the custody sergeant's desk, splitting it open as if it had a zipper, enriching the floor with small red suns. "I'm going to sue the arse off you," he cackles. His lawyer arrives and can barely stand as he thinks of the future litigation.

I am presented to Nikki, who walks in as if she has never seen a police station; she claims me as Rosa's property, the stereo as hers, and last but not least, the earrings (appropriately enough in the shape of the sound of stolen guitars), which she had reported stolen in the first burglary and which have her name engraved on the inside. Whatever his prospects with the police, the Beard is potted for the burgls.

You live in this part of London, you'll never have to pay for entertainment.

Cup of Tea: Sixteen

Rosa is pleased that the culprit has been caught.

Nikki now sits on the floor with the ease of someone who has earned her place in the abode, though she stretches herself with the unease of someone who has overdemanded her muscles.

"Getting in shape?" Rosa asks.

"I was doing cloud-swing today," Nikki says.

"Oh," says Rosa, then decides she might as well ask: "What's that?"

"I do the trapeze."

"You've worked in the circus?"

"Done that. But not actually on the trapeze. I'm not good enough yet."

So this is her mystery sweating.

"Don't you have to start when you're three years old?"

"Not true. I got interested when I went along to a training session and met this guy who was well over forty. I'd watched him and he'd been really good. I was chatting with him and discovered that he'd only been doing it for three years. He'd been a dentist, then one day he decided he wanted to be liked and see people smile when he appeared."

Of course it would appeal to her. Pure flight. She hardly ever feels fear, and when she does she wiggles about on it. Showing death her bottom. Like the bull dancers of Crete, like tumblers everywhere. Strength, speed, sensuality, what else? The only drawback for Nikki is that she doesn't have the patience to make it. The discipline of being in the same place doing the same thing at the same time, however somer-saulty, is beyond her.

It is agreed that Nikki can stay while she works on her act.

A lengthy buzz. Rosa answers.

"Rosa? This is Marius."

"Marius. What a surprise. Come on in."

"Yes, I'd very much like to. But I'm not too well, so I have to ask you first if you have any flu or cold, or if you've sneezed at all this morning. I can't afford another infection."

"Everything's fine."

The collector comes in wearing gloves and a face mask. He still brandishes the fire extinguisher. Nikki inhales money and power and wheels toward him cashtropically. Worry about his collection has brought Marius hither.

"I heard you had burglaries, and I had to make sure everything was okay."

I am produced for Marius to drool over. "I'll take this now," he says. Rosa is not inexperienced in Marius-handling. She closes the door and leans against it before saying:

"I can't let you, Marius. Helen gave it to me, not you."

"You don't trust me?"

"Propriety, Marius. Helen is my employer."

"So, what is it?" inquiries Nikki, wearing only a thin, long, white T-shirt.

My ostensible pedigree is outlined by Marius, as his breathing gains prominence; lust triumphantly rests its foot on the throat of acquisition. Like many old men in the grave up to their noses, he is still chewed by lechery and finds it harder and harder to behave in a seemly fashion. He is slobbering under the face mask, despite needing to strap a splint on his prong to get it up.

"So, is it worth a lot of money?" asks Nikki.

Prognostication: Nikki and I are going to be taking another trip.

"For me, its value is incalculable. But many collectors would pay thousands for it."

I am indeed the gap in his collection. Collections are often shrines for rules. Because we are all paintings, because we are all pots, we belong together. A tidying up of a small square of existence, a little strip of index in the diaspora of being. You probably never finish, but if you do, then what? Woe to the collector with a complete collection. But I understand.

"Wish I had one to sell. You've got an unusual accent. Where are you from?" Nikki simpers, neatly signalling a cash flow with no go in it, and interest. She isn't afraid to use her breasts.

"Originally, Estonia."

Nikki runs my rim with her finger and new respect. "Doesn't look as if it's worth much."

"What do you expect? Dollar signs on the side? This was beautiful when Europe was nothing but a forest, when Egypt was green, when Troy was a couple of fishermen's huts, Athens a few olive trees on a hillside, when the pharaohs were scratching their heads for good building ideas, before the flood. This is the work of a human hand from an age we can't imagine, so different from our own, but perhaps not so different . . . when people still had the same desires. They have always had the same desires. When they wanted to make beauty . . . and to make love."

His voice is breaking up. Nikki must feel pleased that she has her frailest clothing; Marius is trying to look for the faint black triangle without looking as if he's trying.

"You are both so beautiful," he whines. Rosa presumes this is a compliment, a grandfatherly pat, but it's merely standard male preamble. Manners evaporate with money, unless manners are the chosen perversion, and there's nothing like the knowledge that any minute you'll either be too dead or too infirm to feed yourself to help throw respectability to the winds.

"Rosa, if you or your friend would like to earn some more money, I would like to make love to either one of you." He's melting down. He's not expecting a yes; in fact, that is probably the chief pleasure, just having a good disgusting. "Or both of you," he croaks. He could summon a coachload of whores for every meal without noticing the cost. He owns three mountains in Switzerland.

Rosa stares at him with the sort of disgust you can only manage once or twice in your life, her contempt almost throwing Marius against the wall.

"Fine," says Nikki. "Five hundred, all right?"

Marius is disconcerted by this, but he is starting to sweat. Gaping from Rosa.

58

Marius and Nikki depart, Nikki having added a skirt to her body and a pair of boxwood earrings betokening ship-wrecked mariners drawing lots, but fixing it so that the cabin boy gets eaten. I wonder if she knows this. Marius has for-gotten all about getting me in his clutches.

Countryside

Next morning: no Nikki.

Prognostication: She's extracting the gold fillings from Marius's teeth and emptying the sugar bowls, stealing as much as she can carry.

Rosa now loads me into her car.

"I must be on the wrong planet. This has to be a mistake. I'm going to do it. I'm going to do it." She slogans herself up. Her mood clashes with her earrings, which betoken peace, gift-wrapped in red ribbon. The tea caddy where she keeps her jewelry contained other earlore. In her despera-tion, the faience pair, betokening the lone bookshop opened in a backstreet where no one goes (and the few who do ven-ture there are so resolutely indifferent to books that if anyone does actually enter the shop, the proprietor must suspect them of shoplifting) and doomed to a swift out-of-busi-nessing would have been more apt; but desperation is bad for judgement, and perhaps Rosa is right in not wishing to por-tray her soul.

Rosa at the wheel, we're off. I assume I'm to be delivered to Marius. But we head out of town. Marius's country retreat?

We hit a stretch of motorway. Rosa's car is rickety and she proceeds with moderate speed. A truck monsters up next to us in the inside lane, incontestably maintaining an equal speed on purpose. The driver honks and holds up a plaster-board sign—"YOU'RE GORGEOUS" and then "SHOW US YOUR

TITS"—signs prepared earlier and evidently much used to promote mirth and communion on the Queen's highways. The truck driver has face configuration number five hundred and six, the slapped arse. This expression is not of my own invention, I should signal, but one I came across in Moguntiacum; if it's right, it's right. There is a curious relationship between people with faces of this type and transport. Rosa drives on, her eyes glued to the road ahead, missing a third sign, "WE COULD MAKE BEAUTIFUL MUSIC TOGETHER."

With Rosa out of the picture, I re-create Slapped's wife, wife-size, from a snapshot on his dashboard (why carry a picture of a dumpy woman with a snout borrowed from a Berkshire pig and an inability to find a decent hairdresser unless you're forced to?) in the back of Rosa's car where I am. I re-create her waving an admonishing fist. Rosa is so engrossed in ignoring him that she doesn't notice my antics or when Slapped drives off the road to enjoy an accident.

Once every three hundred years or so.

After one hour, forty-six minutes, we stop outside a pleasant but improbably small cottage for a lugal, isolated amid greenery and fields, or at least what passes for isolation at this phase of world history in southern England.

Having emptied the mailbox, Rosa carries me into the cottage. I have become a papoose; whether this is because she is worried about me being stolen again or because she wants to squeeze me for past paste is hard to say. Rosa checks the interior to make sure nothing is amiss and waters some plants. Cat food is dispensed. She is caretaking the property for someone.

Then she takes some bananas and apples out of the fridge and picks up a bottle of mineral water. We go out back and approach a half–falling down shedlike structure. Suddenly I have a horrible fear of a rustic fate, rearing tulips without an appreciative public. Inside the shed I discover that whatever sheddy functions the shed carries out, its principal aim is to prevent access to an old well.

"So?" A voice issues from the well.

Rosa places the fruit and bottle into a bucket and lowers it.

"Oh God," says the voice. It is not the sort of voice you would imagine coming from the bottom of a deep, dark, dank well. It is female, well-groomed, educated, and very mellifluous; this is surprising, since in my considerable experience you wouldn't expect an affluent, educated woman to be so at ease at the bottom of a well.

"Didn't things go well with the blacksmith?"

"No, they didn't," says Rosa.

I remember wondering why Rosa had extricated the ripped-up letter from the bin.

"You know, you shouldn't be expecting too much on a first date."

"I wasn't."

"Oh. You know, I don't mean to complain, I'm sure you've done your best to make things comfortable for me, but it's rather . . . yucky down here. I think I could do a better job helping you if I were at home."

"You're staying where you are until your advice works."

"You know, I'd love to help, but you mustn't forget, I can't work miracles overnight. And you know advice is—how shall I put this? Advice. I can't guarantee anything."

"That's not what you write in your column."

"You're a very passionate and capable person, otherwise you wouldn't be up there and I wouldn't be down here. But there are many people who aren't blessed with your gifts, who need some assurance and guidance about things that might seem very simple to you; there are people who have no one to offer them encouragement, that's why they write to me and that's why people read me; and don't forget, for many people the act of putting pen to paper makes them feel better."

"Talking to you like this makes me feel better."

"I don't want to be difficult at all, but in a certain light, this could look not terribly good, and you might get into trouble for this."

"I wouldn't have thought you'd want it to get out that you ended up down a well because you couldn't even solve one person's problems. And I don't think I'd be much worse off in prison."

"Well, one piece of advice I can give you is that you're unlikely to meet Mr. Right in a woman's jail. Anyway, let's not quibble—verbalize me through the advice you want now."

"I told you."

This is interesting, seeing Rosa in the role of jailer. I wouldn't have spotted it immediately, but of course she has ideals sprouting in her idea plantation; they often produce extremes. She is of the rarest type, Type Five Thousand and Five, a type appropriately that occurs only once in a group of five thousand and five. A type that consequently finds it hard to link. I should have divined it from the petrel-over-Elephant-Island earrings on her dresser.

"I can't help feeling you may be asking for a little too much. The *L* thing isn't something you can go and shop for. You can keep your eyes open and act in a way to encourage them. It could happen next week. It might be a month. Six months. A year. I'm sure I can help you, but you must be patient. The trick is not to worry about being single, but to relish it."

"I'm happy to relish being single, if you're happy to relish dwelling down there, because you're staying there until I'm sorted out."

"What about my family? They'll be worried."

"I've contacted them. Told them you're safe . . . and well. On a retreat. Incommunicado. Not to worry. So, do you have a partner to contact?"

"Not at the moment."

"That's not much of an advertisement for your skills, is it?"

"It's not like ringing for a plumber. I suppose you want someone good-looking, hung like a horse, with a glamorous job, witty, kind to children and animals, to cheer you when you're sad and cheer you even more when you're not, but not to cheer you when you're actually having a bit of fun being sad. Punctual. Never lies. Keen on housework and buying groceries. Insatiable buyer of flowers. Superb cook, but no better than you. Fascinated in the subjects that interest you, and cool on those that don't. So uninterested in other women that he could have three naked Swedish triplets in front of him doing handstands and firing Ping-Pong balls from their pussies and he wouldn't notice."

"Sounds tempting. But that's not what it's about."

This is what has been occupying her. She wants omneity. Rooooosa wants the all-in-one. The unturning. The kiss from which there is no escape. Everyone, even the greatest of lugals, with enough flesh to beast on for a hundred lifetimes, still wants the comfort bringer, the soul harnesser, the splendor mender. Even those with the many want the one.

Is Rosa a fool, searching for perfection? Or a gambler, a daredevil dashing though the crossfire to the ultimate union, not content with half pay? She steps over the sham and the worthless; an authenticator, she wants the authentic. I have lived in these questions for many years, and the answer?

When is prudence cowardice? When it fails. When is insanity bravery? When it succeeds. It is the result that captions the policy: Luck, the fuck.

Few are willing to fight on. Some believe they have arrived when they haven't. Others despair. Rosa's brains make it difficult for her to fool herself. One more feature I hadn't observed fully; by the faint wrinkling of her nose, I educe that Rosa has never made the oooooo machine with a man, for all her perkiness and pertinacity. She is not just looking militantly, she's waiting.

"Honestly, I do think I could be of more use on the surface."

"Advise right and you're out."

"I suppose you should be meeting people. What are you looking for?"

"A man who makes me happy."

"Okay, step one. If you look in my bag, you'll find an invitation to a private showing, it's tonight. Go along. Dress like a whore, the cheaper the better. You can't let your breasts hang out too much. Walk up to the man of your choice once you've checked him out for signs of obvious domesticity; I can give you one absolute rule: Don't even give a married man the time of day. If he's interested, he can hand you the divorce papers. So you walk up to the target; it's no use waiting for men to do anything, they're too timid. You walk up. Big smile. You say you don't know anyone at the party and could you join him? Men love that sort of appeal. And don't forget to make sure that you feel everything he says is wonderful and discuss his doings. There are only about three men in the entire country who don't rate themselves as the most fascinating topic of conversation."

"All right," says Rosa.

"Oh, and one more thing. I don't really want to be the one to tell you this, but the mistake you're making is looking for happiness. What you should be looking for is the right sort of unhappiness."

"I don't remember reading that in your page, Tabatha."

"You can't put it all in."

The marked pages in the pile of magazines back at Rosa's flat now offer meaning. I peer down into the blackness and see that for some reason Tabatha's wearing a pair of earrings representing the smell of mangel-wurzel. I doubt if she knows this. But unwise in choice of earrings, unwise in choice of bottom of wells to be stuck down. All is clear now. Rosa has been plotting this for sometime. She will have lured Tabatha here skillfully. Wise in choice of earrings, wise in skulduggery, as the saying goes, though in Rosa's case, her choice of lobers shows that her heart's not entirely in it.

We go back to the kitchen.

"I help little old ladies across the road. I'm polite and cheery with wrong numbers. I pay my bills on time. I don't litter. I leave water out for the birds when it gets hot. I make a point of recycling everything I possibly can. I give to charities. I don't play music loud, ever, not even during the day. When mail is misdelivered, I promptly remail it, even if it's obviously worthless. When I'm tired of clothes, I take them clean and neatly folded to a charity shop. I let people whom I don't know stay at my flat to help them out. I declare all my income. When my married friends have an emergency, I baby-sit willingly. I give blood. Because I work at home I end up collecting people's parcels for them, letting in their plumbers and builders. I eat carefully. I hardly ever have anything with cream though I love it. I go swimming every other day. I'm told I'm attractive. I'm told I'm good company. I don't want to be rich. I don't want to be famous. I don't want to rule the country. I'm twenty-six and all I want, please, is someone I can love."

Rosa gives a type-sixteen sigh.

"Why can't I find someone who takes it as seriously as me?"

She is pretty, bright, and I know from the way she folds clothes, she is warm of soul. It is confusing when qualities touted as merits don't deliver.

She puts her hands on me, to abscond from the present and to have a go at ago.

Spoiling the Spoils

There was the undying man.

When young, he had been besotted with a maiden. He found her in his every thought. He wooed and proposed to her, but the maiden was someone who wanted to be talked about, and although she was keen on the undying man, she said she could only acquiesce if he visited two hundred places of local interest on his knees, so that when she was married people would point to her and say: Her husband walked on his knees to two hundred places of local interest to win her.

This was an enormous demand, and at first the man refused. She refused to see him anymore. He refused to think about her. This lasted for an afternoon. He pleaded for only fifty places, but she was inelastic. He had the enslavement, so there was nothing to do but to genuflect along, and truthfully, after a few weeks of this, after only twelve places of local interest, he was fed up with it, not to mention his knees, and he thought of giving up, but then he would have suffered in vain; so thinking constantly of her, his manhood in his hand, he kneed on. Besides which, he was becoming a regional celebrity, because everyone who came across him asked him what he was doing, and nearly everywhere he went he got lavish hospitality because people wanted to be able to say the man who went on his knees to two hundred places of local interest had his best meal there.

The ending was not quite as everyone had hoped it would be. When he returned after many months, his sweetheart was already unmissably pregnant by the man she had swiftly married. No one had wanted to tell him.

Enraged and heartbroken, he decided to kill himself. He jumped into a river but somehow couldn't forget how to float and ended up having to walk home from twenty miles downstream, wet, miserable, and hungry, too depressed to try and kill himself again.

The next day he jumped into the river with a number of heavy stones in his pockets. He sank neatly to the bottom of the river, some twelve feet deep, but gradually he noticed that he was breathing air again; he lay down, but the air found him once more. The river had disappeared, its course having been diverted many miles upstream by a tribe wanting to bury its leader in the riverbed and to use the water as an ever-vigilant guardian; he got tired of sitting in the mud and being slapped by fish. He found a rope, tied it to a branch, and jumped. The branch snapped. He found a sturdier branch, and the rope snapped, giving him a nasty burn around the neck. He got a better rope, climbed up the tree, and jumped; the tree uprooted.

He ate dozens of poisonous flowers and berries, and suffered horrifically voiding them. When he had gathered some strength, he went in search of the lair of a notoriously belligerent wild boar. He found the boar snoozing inside and gave it an almighty kick. The boar grunted in displeasure but didn't try to gore him; it went back to sleep. He kicked the boar's rump all the way back to the village, where it was roasted with garlic.

Finally, he went around the village asking someone to behead him. For a fee—all the undying man's possessions—the village shit agreed. The shit got an axe, took a swing, but was laughing so much he missed the man's neck and cut off his own left toes; after that he was too angry to try again.

Then came the invaders.

Looking forward to war, the undying man marched off to battle, naked and dyed blue, wanting to give the enemy every chance of noticing and slaying him. The battle lines were drawn up, and the enemy's champion came forward to taunt them.

He was alpine. Most men could walk between his legs. He was covered from head to toe in armor. He carried a mace the size of a pig, and other fearsome weapons dangled from his belt. Everyone in the front row instantly became very unhappy, and no one felt like trying their luck, except the undying man who strode forward, unarmed apart from a few insults he had memorized in the invaders' language.

Until he was abused, the Champion looked as if he wasn't going to bother killing him. Unusually sensitive about his tentmate, he swung the mace to obliterate the undying man, but it shot off its chain and killed five men in the ranks. The Champion drew his sword, as long and as broad as a bench, and took a stroke at the undying man, who stood still. The Champion shaved several hairs off the undying man's left shoulder but broke his sword in the ground. Annoyed, the undying man stepped forward and bit off the Champion's lower lip, the only exposed part of his body. Shrieking in pain, the Champion ran at him with his dagger but missed, tripped and fell on the dagger, paralyzing himself. The undying man, keenly disappointed, sat on the Champion's face until he stopped breathing.

"Right, you lot. Let's see how good your gods are," he said walking toward the invading army, still armed only with a natural blue dye.

He became the most successful mercenary anyone had ever heard of. He would wear only the lightest of jewelry, and armies all over the region would go into battle, naked, cackling uproariously and carrying flowers, because everyone knew that the undying man went into battle naked (unless it was very cold), cackling, and his preferred method of killing was to cram freshly cut flowers into the mouths of his opponents until they suffocated, while exclaiming, "You're earth!" The armies hoped that the enemy might think he was in their ranks and would be routed in terror.

He was scratched by halberds, his earlobes were clipped by arrows, his beard was trimmed by lances, burning oil singed his eyebrows, dagger thrusts removed morsels of food stuck between his teeth for weeks, spears styled his hair, hatchets cleaned his ears. In forty years of warrioring, the nastiest wound he received was a cut on his left hand from a careless swordsman on his own side during carousing.

Since he won wars, he had to change sides every now and then to keep the fighting going.

At the age of sixty, having survived everyone he had grown up with by twenty years, he saw a girl of thirteen fetching water—an exact double of the woman he had loved, with her innocence and that charm she had had before she became obsessed with places of local interest. He sank to his knees and cried when he saw her because the decades of plunder meant nothing and because it was an era when, due to the popularity of slaughtering, there had not been enough art to provide him with a likeness, so he hadn't seen that glow for forty years. Once he had, the bodies of the women who were waiting for him—adepts at ornamental copulating, their orifices their offices to a woman— were as tasteless and empty as he had always suspected but only now knew.

He asked for her hand immediately, but then pretended to go off on a mortific, and for six months he hired the handsomest, most charming, wittiest beaus to court her, those with the fanciest stringed instruments and greatest knowledge of the fashions to probe her resolution, but she unwaveringly giggled them away. Three days before the wedding ceremony, he caught a cold and died.

As Rosa walks through the vale of the undying man, I can see in her mind, like peaches, pasts waiting to be plucked. This isn't a one-way street.

I extend in and taste one.

It is the highstreet of a thriving economy, with more goods than many countries have in their capitals. She had overheard him say he would be on the highstreet Saturday. Rising early, from nine-thirty until one-thirty she had wandered up and down the highstreet, scanning the faces that poured past, popping into shops, looking at items two or three times.

Store detectives detect her. She is depressed by the clothes; it is not that they don't fit or that she can't afford them, there is simply nothing she likes. She patrols on, clutching the three greetings that she crafted the night before, the readied grappling hooks of conversation. Her legs and soles are aching, when, immediately, he is in front of her, his mouth curved in pleasant surprise.

She gives a swift gift of a smile but walks on purposefully, because although she wants to talk, although she has spent half a day loitering to meet him, she ensures that no one can accuse her of having spent half a day loitering in order to have a coffee with him—by ignoring him.

Five yards away, her sense of stupidity is crushing, but turning back would be even worse, it would definitely reveal her interest in him.

She waits for another hour by the bus stop she knows he should use to return home, judging this to be an acceptable level of coincidence, although he would also know that she didn't live in that direction, she has invented a friend she would be visiting. He doesn't turn up.

Rosa lets goooooo of me. I shoot out of her past like a retracting lizard's tongue.

Her investigations are getting awkward. She's on forty years a day now.

Nikki

Return to the flat: Rosa and I. We find Nikki already returned, struggling with the jar of pickled beetroot.

"And?" says Rosa.

"I'm sorry," says Nikki. "Look, if what I did offended you, I apologize. I wouldn't do that normally, but I really need the money. You know I haven't had any luck getting a job."

"No, it's nothing moral ... it's ... Marius is ... so disgusting."

"Well, wouldn't be any money then, would there?"

"I said you could stay here till you sorted yourself out. Didn't you want to throw up?"

Oddly enough, although the episode has incensed Rosa, somehow the masculine ugliness has brought them together. And there are very few people who don't enjoy a cruise through salacious doings. Nikki can see a subtle hint.

"Nothing much happened in the end. We get in the limo. It's got the smoked, one-way glass. He's shaking like a spin-dryer. Let's go to Oxford Circus, he says. I love doing it in the middle of London, he says. So we start off toward Oxford Circus. Then you can see he's getting worried. He takes me to a clinic where they spend a couple of hours giving me every test you can think of. Everything's fine, apart from an iron deficiency. We go toward Oxford Circus, he's on the phone, ringing people, saying, 'Everything's all right in Japan? No revolution or anything?' Another call. 'Is everything all right in Germany, no revolution or anything?' We get to Oxford Circus, all the shoppers milling around. He's having serious breathing difficulties, so I ask for the cash up front in case he pegs out. I get me clothes off. I go for his zipper. He stops me; he sends his chauffeur for a pair of rubber gloves. I put on the rubber gloves. I go for the zipper. He's wearing ... bullet-proof underwear. No, he says, stop. The rubber might break. Touch yourself, he says. Fine, so I'm stroking me parts and he's doing the same eight feet away from me on the other side of the limo. Put something in yourself, he pleads. I go for a champagne bottle. That works for a bit, but after thirty seconds, he's bored with it. The gun, he says, my chauffeur's gun. I get the gun. No stop, he says, you might shoot me. Take the bullets out. I happily take the bullets out. I start using the gun. He gets bored and then worried. He phones someone up to make sure Frankfurt's still there. He looks at me and says, I want to watch someone make love to you. Fine, I go, but I've been at your disposal since two. You want me to make love to someone, it's another five hundred. Done. Who? His chauffeur? No, he says, My chauffeur is uglier than I am. Get someone good-looking, he says. How am I supposed to do that? I don't know, he says. So I phone a few people. No one around. I might be able to get someone off the street, I say, if I can offer them five hundred. Fine, he says. So I walk up and down Oxford Street for about an hour asking guys if they want to have me and earn five hundred quid. They're quite keen till they hear about Marius. I mean, how shy can guys be? A couple of them would probably kill someone for two hundred. One comes in and has a look at Marius and says no. Another offers me fifty for sex but says he won't do it with Marius watching. Then this really good-looking guy walks up; he's gorgeous, tan, well-dressed. I ask. He says, I could use the money, I want to go on holiday, but, you've guessed it, he's gay. I say I don't mind if you don't. So he climbs into the limo and then Marius says, Who is this guy? I don't know him. We have to check him out. So we make a few phone calls to establish his references, then we take him to the doctor's again. It's getting late. So, we go back to Marius's place—but before he lets us in he suddenly thinks we might be casing the joint so we have mug shots and fingerprints taken and we're blindfolded for the last hundred yards and so we don't see the locks on the door. Inside, there are fire extinguishers and buckets of sand every three yards. What is it with the fire extinguishers, I ask? Spontaneous combustion, he says. Finally, we're back at his bedroom, and my assistant's trying but it's floppy, and I'm not bragging here but you know there are some things I'm good at, and a mouth's a

73

mouth, but it's not happening. I try to be nice, I slap it around. The guy says, Maybe if it were dark I could, you know, imagine you were less . . . female. But then I couldn't see you, says Marius. So we switch off the lights, and the chauffeur nips out for infrared goggles. We get a bit of a bulge. But then it's gone. Perhaps if you cut your hair, he says, you'd look a bit . . . butcher. Marius is ringing up to check Japan hasn't done a runner. All right, I say, I'll cut my hair, but I don't like short hair, that'll be another five hundred. Marius is on the phone, checking that Singapore hasn't sunk and calling for a doctor. You hate me, says Marius. No, I don't hate you, Marius, I say, you're fuhking disgusting, but I don't hate you. Why doesn't anyone like me? he wails. You're revolting and you obviously don't give a shit about anyone but yourself, I say. His jaw drops. I don't think many people have told him that lately."

Doubtless Nikki didn't spare the contumely since she is clever enough to know that Marius is a one-transaction man; there will be no repeats, no chance to wind her way into his confidence, no chance to come back and slip items into her pockets because the staff will frisk her on the way out.

"I think I'm going to get another five hundred for insulting him but finally, bingo. We call Mr. Droopy's boyfriend in to provide the horn. We have to have him checked out, but finally he sashays in, abracadabra. Like he's got a dachshund welded on. He gives it to me royally. I scream and scream. Marius has been asleep. We argue over the money. I didn't see it, he says. Listen, we weren't paid to keep you awake as well, I say. Funny thing is, I've had sex with lots of gay guys. . . ."

"What?"

"I had a phase when I was right off men. Straight men—they were so unreliable, and if they weren't taking your money, they were slapping you around. I was working as a stripper—I was just sick of them pawing me; it's not a profession that makes the male of the species seem endearing. I lived with three gay guys, and you know, Saturday night when there's nothing on television and you haven't got the money to go out and it's raining. You get bored. I always regretted it; I nearly always went to hospital afterward."

Nikki stops here, realizing that their newfound amity might not be able to take this wealth of copulatory detail. I can guess what solution she found to save wear and tear on that unyieldingest of orifices: By providing facilities for the double dick trick, her pussy as conference center. I had a design like that which gained me a great following in the Gupta empire. People kept killing each other over me before I called it a day.

"Have you . . . er, you know . . . for money before?"

Nikki draws up one leg onto her chair to rest her chin on it.

"Wasn't the first time. It's nothing I'm ashamed of. I did it when I needed money for my mother's operation. It's a way of making money, that's all. I didn't mention it because some people have an odd attitude toward working girls; they think you must be on the needle and a liar and a thief just because you're on the game."

They round off the evening by the-most-inane-or-inexpert-opening-or-leg-spreading-line-from-a-man competition:

Nikki: "Anything you find in my trousers is yours."

Rosa: "Do you know you have fuck-me-sideways ears?"

Nikki: "Have you got a map of the world?"

Rosa: "I'm doing a survey: How do you feel about being chatted up in the street?"

Nikki: "I've slept with everyone else in the house."

Rosa: "How about lunch?"

75

Nikki doesn't see why this is outrageous, but Rosa explains she was naked in the bathroom at the time, and it came from a man whom she had never seen before who had climbed in through the window.

Nikki, I notice, surreptitiously peeks at me with a deep wistfulness.

"It's scary," says Rosa, looking at the empty bottle of vodka between her and Nikki. "I was thinking of the first boy I was in love with, when I was fourteen. It's almost like someone else's life. I can't remember what he looks like. His face is there, but it hardly has any features."

"I don't know why you're worried about that," says Nikki. "I can't remember the faces of the guys I fuhked last year." She scratches her armpit richly.

But the past is there. It is only in that four-letter verb that Nikki nakedly reveals her origins. Within thirty miles of Leicester. Her time in Barcelona and Berlin is also there, but I doubt anyone but me would notice it. And even I find it hard to keep up with all the mutations. A hundred years ago I would have been able to name the street where Nikki grew up.

"We're all trying to find the unfindable, aren't we?" Rosa remarks, the extreme consumption of alcohol always provoking tumbling adages. Although I have spent hundreds of years as a drinking vessel—I've done the skyphos, the rhyton, the oxybaphon, the pentaploa, the plemochoe, the philotesia, the kothon, the kantharos, the elephas, and the deinos—I don't approve of it at all.

"Trying to book the unfindable room," murmurs Rosa.

This is remarkable. I don't know why mortality afflicts mortals so much. They always come back from a roam in the loam. The same mannerisms, the same hairstyles, the same laughs, the same conversations; indeed, sometimes the same expressions. A new nose or a different color perhaps, but otherwise business as usual. At any moment in the world, millions of people will be having the ten unceasing conversations that flit around like gnats from house to house, country to country, and back again. At this moment, more than one interlocution will be about frozen iguanas.

Odile

The unfindable room was one Odile always used to say. Or to be precise, she said it one hundred and nineteen times. "All the answers. I know where they are. Whatever it is you are looking for, wherever you are in the world, it is in the same place, the unfindable room."

The line she said only once was: "But the problem with the unfindable room, as you may have guessed, is that it is unfindable; you cannot find it, it can only find you."

The bouncing ball was another Odile-ism. She said it two hundred and fifteen times in my hearing. The bouncing ball was one of her theories, but one that couldn't ever be proved. Her idea was that even if you dropped a ball in exactly the same conditions, it would never bounce in exactly the same way twice, partly because once a ball had bounced, you could never debounce it. And if you tried to make identical balls, they might look similar, but they wouldn't be exactly identical. And even if God made you two guaranteed-identical balls, they wouldn't bounce the same. Still, she spent a loooooot of time dropping balls and lumps of rubber. She felt that what looked like rules, weren't. They were just there to get you off guard. Nature was sheepish and would allow itself to be herded, but one or two sheep would always wander off.

There haven't been many people I've liked, because there aren't many likable people. There have been a large number,

77

but let's not get into figures here—approximately four hundred thousand whom I've had no serious objection to or major grouse about. But people I've liked: thirty. Of the collectors, none come close to Odile; even the least odious among them shouldn't have been allowed to pedicure her.

"Neck-handled amphora. Attic Geometric. Circa 840 B.C." were her first words to me. And indeed, that was precisely the style and shape I was using, though to be absoooooolutely accurate, it was the winter design of 843 B.C., but not bad for a twelve-year-old girl getting a birthday present in Tallinn in 1834 when the pottery of the ancient world had barely been rediscovered and dusted off from graves in Etruria.

But Odile was sharp. And as hard to handle as she was smart. When she set off for London at the age of fourteen, completely against her parents' wishes, they insisted on her being accompanied by two cousins and three governesses, noted for their vitality, endurance, and physical strength, who were offered unprecedented bonuses if they succeeded in sticking to her. She liked difficulty. I and eleven other cumbersome pieces of pottery were transported with her; she traveled collected.

Her English was already fluent by the time she arrived there; within a year only a handful of educated people had a greater command than she. For months she wandered in the most seedy and dingy areas of London, causing amazement and perplexity with her questions. She wrote a novel in English about a young orphan raised in a workhouse who falls in with child pickpockets in London's underworld. She sent it off to various booksellers the week before a Mr. Charles Dickens started serializing a novel called *Oliver Twist*.

We move to Manchester where she again throws herself into examining the lives of the poor, doing good works and ruminating on social order. She compiles a book on the throstle, hosiery, pottery, false weights, factory hands, lace and calico, miners, incendiarisms, and the workhouse. She had just prepared a fine copy of this work in her own hand when a friend from Germany sends her a newly published book by a Herr Friedrich Engels, *The Condition of the Working Class in England in 1844*; Odile reads German and her friend thinks she might be interested in the book.

We pack our bags and barouche to Paris where she is involved in the revolution, though I never find out exactly how, since I and the other breakables are packed out of harm's way and she never talks about it. Dandies in the salons are horsewhipped by her wit, and several flee Paris, never to return; distinguished writers are unable to supply answers to her inquiries about the intricacies of French grammar and syntax. She commits four years to writing a novel about a young farmer's daughter who marries a doctor in Normandy. The heroine has a number of unsatisfactory affairs and finally takes arsenic obtained from an apothecary. Odile traveled into Paris from her country retreat, where she had completely cut herself off to mold the manuscript, to seek a publisher the week after the first installment in the *Revue de Paris* of a novel called *Madame Bovary* by a Monsieur Gustave Flaubert.

This was the decisive blow for Odile's literary endeavors. Not one to sulk, however, we immediately depart for the East. To take time off from her writing, Odile had always had a keen interest in zoography; she was always popping insects and unfortunate organisms into jars of alcohol, sketching birds, and bringing magnifying glasses to bear on spiders. The travels are fraught, and I speak as someone who has tasted a varied selection of shipwrecks and ambuscades.

I rarely tamper.

I decided that shelf-sitting is the best policy after a nurse dropped a newborn infant into me, jar that I was at the time, and replaced my lid, expecting me to carry out the office of executioner. I immediately opened up some airholes. The squalling infant grew up to be a superlugal and to massacre thousands in a sparsely populated region, in the most lurid manner, germinating pain a million times greater than the one I had diverted.

Odile's gallivanting: One night in the Pacific, some sailors were harboring unnatural and natural lusts toward Odile and wanted to wait for her in her cabin. As one came in, I grew to ten feet in size and showed him a leaping Bengal tiger, life-size, life-detailed, even the fleas, everything except the smell and the noise (don't let anyone tell you that the motion picture was invented by the French)—something that caused him a severe crisis in his interpretation of the world and to dismiss all thoughts of wrongdoing; as soon as he managed to compose himself he threw himself overboard. This was my fifteenth intervention in fleshy fortunes.

In Australia, making constant reference to her bottled bugs and floating lizards, Odile works ceaselessly on a treatise seeking to explain the creation of different species. She sends her work to London, where it arrives a fortnight after a paper by a Mr. Charles Darwin is presented to the Linnaean Society, expounding his theory of natural selection, a theory, in my opinion, which lacks the color and humor of Odile's account.

In Geneva, Odile finally decides to give rein to much-postponed yearnings. No longer young, she still bags a Russian count. Applying her considerable intellect to the act, she gives the Count a preview of marital pleasures. Not a man unfamiliar with coition, the Count is unable to fathom how any woman could do such things; certainly Odile used one or two touches I had never encountered before (presumably they had been invented in a Parisian bawdyhouse two weeks earlier). The Count loses two teeth biting off a wooden butterfly carved on one of the bedposts, his tool having become a racetrack for joy; he proposes with a bloody and splintered tongue.

They retire to the Count's estate just outside of St. Petersburg, where Odile takes up economics once more, studying local factories and working her way through digests. She produces a six-hundred-page work outlining a theory of surplus value and accumulation of capital. About as interesting as dusting, as far as I'm concerned. The morning she puts the final full stop to the manuscript, she receives from her German friend now living in London a copy of *Das Kapital* by a Herr Karl Marx. *Adieu* economics.

Back to science. She assembles a talking phonograph and proudly waits to show it to her husband, who returns from St. Petersburg with a magazine carrying the news of a Thomas Edison and his machine. She dies in 1890 with a pile of paintings of curiously distorted objects and people that none of the art pundits in St. Petersburg would even look at, a series of shallow glass dishes with glorious molds, and a manuscript with the title of "The Joseph Device for the Calibration and Deciphering of Dreams as Related to an Individual's Health"; the manuscript is covered with a stack of rejection letters from grandees saying that they cannot give serious consideration to work by someone without the proper academic background.

But her collections always gave her pleasure. She had two great collections, the ceramics . . . and the mad poets.

She had a small asylum built on the estate. Why she chose mad poets, I can't depuzzle entirely, but if you collect, I suppose you have to specialize, and, if you are as interested in studying them as Odile was, they have the advantage of writing down some of their own ramblings. And as she said, "They're God's amanuenses"—struggling to reinstate the language of Babel. I could have told her a few stories about that, but never mind.

Yes, she was a real collector, the sort only a collector collector could appreciate. Every morning she rose before dawn to go and briskly inspect her stable of barking bards, snatched from the garrets, gendarmeries, and bedlams of Europe; she would feed them fresh fruit and vegetables grown all year round in her greenhouses and collect the verses produced overnight.

The verses weren't always plentiful. There was the Welsh poet who would sleep all night and most of the day, rising only to eat and to maintain that "you can't rush a good poem." So much so that in the fifteen years he was there, he never produced a single verse, behavior one might say not so untypical of men of letters adjudged sane and celebrated in their countries; the Welshman however would reply "you can't rush a good poem" to any question or anything you might you say to him, occasionally changing it to "a good poem, it can't be rushed."

There was Sven, whose surname was unknown and who had been shipped to us from a Swedish port. He was the most prolific of the bedlamites: He wrote sonnets, pindarics, ghazals, villanelles, rondels, sestinas, fatras, blasons, epithalamions, planhs, and unconvincingly short epics, which were essentially the same two couplets eulogizing carnal congress with thirteen-year-old girls; the only noticeable differences between the various productions was the number of times the girls' names were repeated, the occasional change in the names (three phases, Babette, Sølvi, and Karen), and mutations in the orthography. These effusions were part of a grand theosophical scheme—namely that Sven was sure that when he died, God would grill him: "So Sven, how many thirteen-year-old girls did you deflower?" The whole universe, according to Sven, was an elaborate obstacle course keeping the aspirant from passing through the maidenly hoops to salvation. This was the great secret that few knew and even fewer acted on. Thus he viewed the madhouse as a masterful snare erected by the forces of evil to prevent him from reaching the elect.

"And women?" asked Odile.

"That's your problem. The dickless are those who fared badly in previous lives."

"And if you happened to be a thirteen-year-old girl and you deflower yourself?"

"The teachings are vague on this point."

Her star acquisition was an expensive purchase from a leading German bin, since the Germans had been reluctant to let such an interesting case go. The poet who wrote in what he called invisible ink, since he didn't want anyone stealing his ideas; most of us would have termed it nonexistent ink, since the ink existed only in his mind. He moved his bone-dry quill over the pages with the alacrity of a scratching dog. The interesting part was that if you removed his work and tried to insert identical sheets of virgin paper, he could tell and would begin to scream that the paper was blank, or if you returned a series of invisibly written papers out of order, he would complain.

There were a number of poets who I also suspect were not mad or even severely eccentric, but were lured to Odile's by the prospect of free lodging and grub. "Good morning, madame, I'm a poet and I'm mad, mad, and mad," the big-eared Georgian introduced himself and tried to grab Odile's breasts. Odile rearranged her earrings and had two of the servants thrash him senseless. "Okay. Okay, you don't know what you're missing," he said, straightening his broken nose. "What's for supper? I've come a long way."

"You're not mad. You're bad," she said, returning his manuscripts.

"No, no. I'm mad, I should know: I live with myself all the time."

"It's not usual for the mad to want to get into a madhouse."

"That shows that I'm a hopeless case."

Big Ears handed her another selection of long verses on how women had sold their best family jewelry for only a few hours of his company. A villonade depicted him catapulting a salt cellar twelve feet with the passionate erectness of his member. "You're mad if you think you're going to get anywhere like that," said Odile.

"I told you so," he said, taking off his clothes again. She had the servants throw him against a wall for half an hour.

"I tell you what," said Odile, "I'll give you a thousand rubles if you leave and promise never to write poetry again."

"I couldn't do it for less than five hundred."

"I said a thousand."

"Okay. Two hundred and fifty. My grandmother's very sick."

"Nice try. The thousand stands."

It was a big-blow battle between greed and vanity. Big ears took the money. "Truth is, I'm too old for this lark. I only did six feet last week."

"Take the salt out."

"Madame, I have my dignity."

Some duds did slip in. Odile had some frauds foisted on her. For instance, the mad poet who revealed himself to be a mad critic. He would demand the work of the invisible composer and then scan it solemnly before declaring: "How underivative, how unshallow, how unwooden, how unmonotonous." The mad poet next door would foam in rage, "How dare you praise my work? You obviously haven't read it properly or you would see how worthless it is!" The mad critic was tubby and would snore loudly. The poets would collect rhinoliths and would propel them into the critic's open mouth.

Odile sent a large sum to an Italian asylum in Naples that claimed to be offering her a Japanese poet, at that time a bit of a sensation. The money said to be merely for transport costs. She thought she had been gulled, but two years later a gnarled-footed scarecrow with enough calluses to make a suit of armor arrived carrying the map that he had been given at the asylum, which consisted of Naples and then somewhat above it, Russia. A Slovenian, he wasn't strictly speaking a poet or indeed a writer: He painted letters. At first they were small, pencil-painted letters he liked the look of, rather like those letters that appeared on the Tyrrhenian vases and that so many people have found so puzzling. But his letters grew bigger and he gave them titles such as *The Letter A at the Age of Ten*, or *The Letter S Reflects*, *The Letter T from the Back*. The final development was his painting letters in dressing gowns, wearing jack boots, and my favorite, the most impressive—*The Letter B Wearing the Letter L's Clothing Without the Letter L Knowing About It*.

Another deceptive acquisition was a choleric baldie from Minsk who had obvious literary hankerings but who on examination turned out to be a mad publisher. He swore a lot, and it took a while to piece together his story, but he maintained that he had recollection of his previous lives and in every incarnation he had been a purveyor of letters.

"Homer—imbecile. Bleater. He was singing around

85

campfires for scraps of food when I found him. Gratitude? My arse. Hesiod—imbecile. I had to correct everything. Sophocles? Boring. Bleater. Couldn't you liven it up a bit? I said. I pleaded with him, but would he listen? Ovid? Bleater. Always late. Dante—imbecile. Couldn't spell. Shakespeare? Shakespeare? Thick as two short planks, and I had to give him all the ideas. Goethe? Grumbler. Don't even mention him. Bleating, all of them. It can be a clear, still summer night, but you can hear it, hear it in the distance, getting closer and closer, the bleating. They've got too little money to write. Give them a coin. They've got too much money to write. Take it away, they have too little."

None of the authors he handled brought him any pleasure except the Avar, Mmmmmm, whose works he insisted he had handled in the Dark Ages and were the greatest of all. He always yelled for paper so he could write down Mmmmmm's work. "Mmmmmm, what a gentleman! Such charm! Such wit! Such passion! Such appealing erudition! Such goodness! Such variety!" But it never happened.

Odile trawled through histories and studies and wrote letters to learned folk in the region, who could offer no knowledge of the aforementioned poet. But she kept on giving the mad publisher paper. "What if he isn't mad?"

There was another reincarnationist. Local lad. He could remember two thousand previous lives: The countries weren't always the same, but in all of them, as in his present life, he was a carpenter, his name was Yakov, or Jacob, or Giacobbe, or Jake; his wife's name was Eve, or Eva, or Ewa, or Evita; and he always got lentils for breakfast, lunch, supper, and snacks. He was extremely depressed by this and would just lie around, unable to take any interest in life. "Don't bother to wake me," he'd say, lying down. Even the excellent cuisine didn't cheer him up. "I'll be back on the lentils soon." "I'd kill myself, but there'd be no point. You know I've made the same chair ninety thousand times."

Odile took him in, because locals couldn't understand her predilection for metrical mania and had presented him to the asylum. We also acquired the self-eater.

He had been the best-looking mujik in the village. Miller. He had married the best-looking girl. They had the best-looking children in the village in the best-looking house. Then one day the mujik's wife came to see Odile, distressed, seeking help. "It started with his bottom lip. It went one day; he said he had bitten it off accidentally, chopping wood. Then his top lip went, and he said again it was chopping wood. Then his fingers started going; I suppose I should have been suspicious when I found one cooking in a stew I was preparing."

"He's eating himself?"

The wife burst into tears.

His fingers, earlobes, toes, and left arm—deserted one by one. This might have been explained by a remarkable accident-proneness, but the severed items were never found. Odile went to visit and found the mujik at the stove, frying. Spluttering in the frying pan was his dick, which had made the women's faces for fifty miles around go funny shapes. "It was a tough decision. But I've got three wonderful kids. I'd offer you some, but there's not enough to go round."

They offered him a meal up at the estate, but he ran off en route. A few nights later his wife was woken up by him. He had cut off his left leg. "You do it for me, dear. You know I can't cook." His mobility greatly diminished, he was conducted to the poet collection. "You're not fooling anyone. You just want it all for yourself. You've no right to come between a man and his leg. I've earned that," he insisted. He was the only one of the bedlamites to escape. He didn't get far; he was found in the kitchen, his other leg carbonized in the oven; he had lost so much blood cutting it off that he had passed out and burned the gigot of miller.

"Why do you do it?" Odile asked.

"No, no, the question is why aren't you doing it? You're just jealous because I thought of it first. You haven't lived."

The village cripple who had lost both legs in the war drowned himself in the pond, weighted down with a couple of Bibles.

Odile did have some success. Success: Using color methods, she gradually disabused the mad publisher of his tirades and helped him to remember that he in fact was a teacher of French from a small town.

Thanks: "You bitch," he reproached, "I was the greatest bookseller in history and now I can I go back to an obscure town where the biggest laughs come from vegetables in funny shapes. I can now look forward in the remaining years of my life to trying to teach irregular verbs to twelve-year-old dunces who couldn't learn them even if I had the opportunity of using the rack and the knout as pedagogical incentives, and earning enough to eat dry bread. That's if I'm lucky. I predict that I won't even be able to get that exciting work, since everyone knows me as the madman, and there's nothing less likely to attract invitations to instruct their gormless treasures than insanity. I'll probably starve to death in two months. If I'm unlucky, I might stretch it out to two years. You cured my madness, but you can't cure my life."

Other unsuccesses: "Pots don't betray," Odile said. "A vase won't decamp. An amphora won't change its mind about you. You don't find a krater wandering off into someone else's arms. A stamnos won't make a cutting remark about your dress. Pelikes won't not write to you from abroad. You leave an aryballos on a dresser, it'll be there when you get back."

Her husband was more interested in animal husbandry and emptying vodka bottles. He was drunk round the clock and imported Georgian floozies by the coachload. "You have your studies. I have mine." He was depressed, to be fair, having realized that his life's achievements as grayness settled on him was having drunk a lot and having worked out what his manhood was for, which even among the idleness of the aristocracy was fairly inconsequential.

"What will become of you?" she said to me on her deathbed. She was worried that we would come to an unworthy finale. Her concern was great, even for the inanimate. There were few people like Odile who could look life in the face with curiosity, good humor, and unfailing resolution. As she lay in laudanum, I played some great scenes for her; the greats greating, things no humans had seen for thousands of years, rhinos on the Seine, creatures no one of her generation could ever see, because I knew she would appreciate the show.

"The vase is talking to me," she would say to the servants, who, of course, nodded in agreement.

Her husband communicated his best wishes through the doctor. He didn't come to see her for the three weeks she was abed because he couldn't bear the sight of illness. He didn't go to the funeral either, because he found funerals depressing.

Even Odile, stockpiler of wisdom, who rode brilliance as far as it could go, couldn't get the marriage right.

Restaurant

I'm in the bag.

Rosa has been running over the terrain of her face, plucking, charting, squeezing, embellishing; it was a long afternoon in the bathroom, a long time staring into the wardrobe. She picked up the earrings with the spirals that represent learning with great difficulty and humiliation over several months the rudiments of a foreign language in anticipation of someone attractive you met abroad coming to visit but then never hearing again from that attractive person. Rosa didn't know that, but she sensed it. She saw a pair of Nikki's lobers: high-speed car chase. She tried them on; they worked for her.

We are waiting for a man. Not one produced by Tabatha's advice, but a late letter. I wonder whether this evening will spring Tabatha from the well. Rosa attempts to drink her water in the manner of someone who has stashed an agony aunt in a well and isn't showing it, but all she achieves is the manner of someone who has stashed an agony aunt in a well and is trying not to show it, but does.

The bag is positioned by Rosa's leg. Entrance of the man: tall, intelligent, educated, blade-nosed. Hair not at the height of fashion, but too early to say whether this is because he scorns vogue and prefers his own trail or is merely unaware that things have moved on. He gives the smile of a man who knows he knows how to make women pant. Yes, a portion of arrogance, but there are hardly any women who don't have a taste for some thrashing conceit.

Teacher: not a good sign. Few people go into this profession because they want to. They're failed somethings—bank robbers, conductors, pilots, people who never found the way out of the educational system. A teacher of English to foreign students: even worse. Someone whose only employable trait is having been born in a country where the language happens to be in demand. In a teachery style, he talks with the expectation of being listened to. But you have to wonder why a strapping guy with all his own teeth and hair and some sort of income is out in the market at thirty-two?

Rosa takes it in; she is doubtless already imagining herself being tied to the bed with silk scarves, naming children, wondering how fat he'll be at fifty. She gives him half a dozen costume changes as she unfolds her napkin. Having counted on a lumbering halfwit, explosively she clears a path to her heart. You can see her thinking: about time.

"Perhaps," he says, as she raises a glass of wine, "you'd like to congratulate me on my choice of wine."

Rosa smirks. She thinks this is a joke. I can spot it a long way before she does. She is busy rehearsing strigiling him with her tongue. This is not a man who is going to make women happy; he may make a few nuke but he's not going to make them happy, nor is he going to make them unhappy in an interesting or enriching way; he is a minor exasperator. His choice of wine isn't remarkable, and I should know; but anyway, in a half-decent restaurant you're not going to get a bad wine. Mr. English talks. A lot. About himself. The waiter attempts to take the orders three times and is hustled away by English, who hasn't even looked at the menu, so busy is he unfurling his flag. The jobs, the demand, the ovations. Rosa begins to get the picture. The odd thing is he clearly knows he's a dud, he's not fooling himself; but perhaps that's what he's looking for rather than real success, someone who believes he's a real success, even if it's only for a few hours. One hour in, Rosa has said thirty words, and that includes her order and saying thank you twice to the waiter who brought the food.

I watch them eat, without much interest. Eating is an oversubscribed activity. Every creature on the planet is trying to persuade the rest of the planet into its stomach. Mouths chasing mouths to remouth them. Gnats, rats, meerkats, bureaucrats racing to gnat, rat, meerkat, and bureaucrat the world. Eaters become eater eaters who become eater-eater eaters who become eater-eater-eater eaters who become eater-eater-eater-eater eaters. Very quickly. And they say there's no such thing as progress.

"They didn't want to let me go, but China's too small for me, really, and I had been given this offer to run a school in Denmark by an old friend." The waiter, somehow sensing Rosa's torture, brings the bill without the request of Mr. English. Relief expands all over Rosa. "You must be thrilled to be here with me," he says. "Don't be shy. Say so anytime." He pauses to take a much-needed glass of water.

"Don't you want to ask something about me?" says Rosa. "Aren't you curious?"

"Yes, there is something I'd like to ask you. Could I take a picture of you?" Rosa exposes some teeth, which could pass as agreement. He whips out a Polaroid and takes a snap. "I can't believe what a brilliant choice this restaurant was," he says as he shakes the picture to speed its desiccation. He reaches for an album. "I know you'll want to write something about how thrilling the evening's been."

The faces in the album: a round-faced blonde, lumbering make-up, smiling from ear to ear, strawberry-cheeked, holding up a glass of champagne, too young, too sozzled to be bothered, only a few dozen dinners on the clock. Her inscription: *Cheers.*

A square-faced, pointy-eared French osteopath unable to believe she had walked into this: *Unforgettable.* Dark-eyebrowed lexicographer, sinking fast, wielding the slogan, don't give up, don't give up: *What an evening!* A grinny Brazilian, finding things amusing, experienced lips, a passport huntress who isn't going to be distracted by the fact he's solid oaf: *When I am going to see your little friend?*

Rosa writes: *Unbelievable.* You wonder what the point is; he's too intelligent to really fool himself, and he's hit the album this early because he knows he won't be getting another look. Out comes his calculator, and he starts to work out Rosa's contribution. Rosa wants to end it by blanketing it with cash, but he demurs: "We've got to get it right."

Good-bye: "Tell all your friends about me," he urges.

"Don't worry."

What is the purpose of despair? Pain for the brain? If you are a type five thousand and five, the odds are not hopeless, but enough to make it difficult, enough to feel an Alpinist in the Sahara.

Back at the flat, Rosa unloads to Nikki, who is in her leggings and is doing various exercises on the floor for suppleness and strength.

Strange Men Competition

Rosa serves up the Dinner Flopperist.

"Why not have a florida anyway? One night they're pretty much the same," opines Nikki.

"No."

"Though it's terrible when you think you've got a hot property and you get him home and it's no-go. It's like buying a blouse and discovering a hole or it's dry-clean only. There was one hulking guy I got back, and he's got this motorbike collection so we look at pistons for about two hours, 'cause you've got to humor them a bit, and I say this has been fascinating, could we get our clothes off? We get our kit off, and I'm all ready to go and he's floppy, so I say, Let me get you hard, and he says I *am* hard, but it's just like the head, nothing else. Like he's lost the rest or something, it's two inches, max. You don't need a marrow obviously, and for all I know dinkiness might do it for some women; honestly, if it's that small I feel you should give some warning. Hand out a card or something, so you can make up your mind whether you want a go or not. It'd be quite enticing if a guy gave you a card saying 'Two inches, at your disposal.' Wouldn't you want to have a look?"

"Maybe."

"Mind you, the strangest ones were the ones I came across when I was on the game. There was one guy who used to come up, pay up, and then start reading from the Bible. So what do you think happens next?"

Rosa shrugs.

"Nothing. That's it: He reads to me for five minutes. I thought it was his way of getting the juices going. But no, that was it. Money, quick read of the Bible while I did my nails. And nothing preachy about hussies roasting in eternal brimstone. I don't think it was a dick kick."

"Hmmm."

"A lot of them weren't into sex. And the sex was often the easiest bit. The hardest part was having to be nice and laugh at their jokes, make small talk. And they weren't all beer-bellied accountants from Birmingham. I had one quite good-looking one. He just wanted me to do what he said. Stand up. Sit down. Roll over. Make a cup of tea. Down we'd go to Leicester Square and I'd have to crawl after him, begging for it. 'Please, Micky, please, I need it. You were fantastic. Please. You're the only man who's ever made me come. Beat me if you want.' Oh, but I'm forgetting the icing, I had to do all this, but I had to do it in front of French tourists. That was the tough part, making sure they were French. Belgians or

Swiss wouldn't do. He had this thing about Frenchwomen, but he was stingy. We had a big fight 'cause we'd been waiting for half an hour. Can you believe it, in the middle of London you can't find some Frenchwomen? But he wouldn't pay to keep the meter running."

"Hmmm."

"Wait, the best one of all was the car-park fancier. How could I forget him? This woman turns up one day, very respectable, middle-aged, and I think, Fine, your money's as good as anyone's, but she wants to bring her husband. He's been caught in car parks, rubbing himself on the ground. Urban developments seem to do it for him. She's in tears 'cause he's been arrested in a shopping center in the middle of the night, wearing only a pair of socks, giving it to the paving. It turns out he's been at it for years—while he was abroad on business. He's shagged the Eiffel Tower, World Trade Center, the Prado. Given the Taj Mahal a good seeing-to. He'd always been deported. Then he's caught getting his leg over in the fast lane of the M25 one night. He's running out of employers and countries to visit. No cathedral's safe. His wife can't let him out of the house 'cause he'll drop 'em and go to work on the nearest pavement—the bigger the audience, the bigger the kick. She sent him to a shrink but discovered he was only going along because there was a good-looking car park next to him, with which he had his evil way. She tried everything and hoped a professional might take the heat out of his activities. She didn't want him to have any emotional attachment, just to shag it out. A case of her wanting him to shag the woman next door, rather than next door."

"And?"

" 'Course it didn't work. I tried. Really straight-looking guy. Gold-club joiner. But his wick only burned for wide-open concrete. You know, I can offer some fun. But he just gave me the money and told me to tell his wife we were hard at it. Last I heard, he was off trying to give the Kremlin one."

"So who was the worst customer?"

"The worst customers, I'd say, the really disgusting ones were the ones who didn't turn up. There's nothing more infuriating than a no-show. There was this guy, African, who'd phone up and explain how he had this enormous sexual organ and could we cope with it? Then we'd have a half-hour discussion about the price, we'd try and make it clear that there was no negotiation, but he didn't believe us, he kept on saying that we'd enjoy it so much, a third of the normal rates should apply. He didn't understand the nature of the business. Then he wouldn't turn up, then there'd be another half-hour conversation while we attempted to direct him the two hundred yards from the phone booth to our flat; he just couldn't make it. Chief Log we called him; he could have represented his country in stupidity. I went down to look for him once, but he'd wandered off somewhere; he was probably frightening every female in a mile radius. Then there'd be those who'd call up for you to visit, and by the time you got there they had fallen asleep or changed their mind. I spent an hour driving out to the bloody countryside once at two in the morning. I had a bad feeling about it, but I needed the money; I got to this pub, the guy was the landlord, and I rang and rang, nothing; he'd obviously flaked out. So I rang for the fire brigade, an ambulance, and the police and then I started waking up the neighbors, saying, 'I'm sorry to disturb you, but I'm a prostitute who's come down from London for Mr. Howard and I'm very worried that something terrible has happened to him.' They broke the door down and found him snoring away, and then looking a trifle perplexed at seeing us all there."

"Mmmmm."

"Don't let it get you down. It happens. When I was on the game, I made some good money, but afterward I spent six months without an offer; all someone had to do was ask nicely, but no. You should try the ladder."

"The ladder?"

"I had to change a lightbulb once, but I couldn't reach. I went round the corner to borrow this ladder, and I was carrying it back when this guy volunteers to carry it for me; and let's cut a short story shorter, he volunteered a lot more. It's worked since. Men like it 'cause they can act strong and superior, and they can never think of anything to say when they fancy you. You should try it; it attracts the healthy, considerate type; if you don't like the look of him you can always get huffy and say you can manage."

"Hmmm."

Nikki bends her head down to her knees. "Uuuuuummfff. That hurts. It's always hell when you've been out of practice. But I'm getting stronger. I ought to think about getting a routine together."

A program on the new television about women on women. It gets to bedtime.

"Look, I know this sounds rather odd, and you can say no, but I'm feeling a bit insecure. I couldn't sleep in your bed tonight, could I?" inquires Nikki.

"I wouldn't be able to sleep," says Rosa. I am taken into her bedroom as usual and placed under the duvet. But tonight Rosa moves her makeup seat and places it against the door. She puts her hands on me. Return of the gone. I give her the story of the collector who didn't want to be a collector but had collectoring forced on him.

Countryside

We go out again, check the cottage, and go to the well.

"So?"

"I went to the party. I went up to the best-looking man, who was really good-looking, and guess what I said to him?"

" 'I don't know anyone here, do you mind if I join you?' "

"Correct. Guess what he said."

"Oh, I don't know: 'Delighted to meet you. Did you hurt yourself when you fell from heaven?' "

"No. What he said was: 'You're plainly a gate crasher. I have to ask you to leave.' "

"Oh."

Rosa lowers the bucket.

"I don't mean to complain, but I'm getting a little tired of being down this well. I do have a life of my own."

"Fix me up."

"What about your supper? Weren't you supposed to be having a supper?"

"Don't even ask."

"I can't believe it. You know, I think you should concentrate on enjoying being single more. The watched flower never blooms. You're trying too hard."

"It's nothing to do with me. Advise, that's your job. Advise."

Despite the harshness of her response, Rosa is softening. Her incarceration of Tabatha is a borrowing of others' behavior, just as she borrowed Nikki's earrings. Again, the idea that behavior makes a difference, just as an unsuccessful gambler will change his lottery numbers.

"I'm obviously not exteriorizing right. I've told you I think I could be a lot more effective if I wasn't stuck here. I could make some introductions."

"Your castoffs."

"If you're asking for help, don't complain when you get it."

"If I get it, I won't complain."

"I still don't entirely understand why you felt it necessary to go to these lengths.... How shall I verbalize this? Why me?"

"That's what I find myself saying. If I might quote from one of your replies: You don't have to change your life, just your way of thinking."

"I wonder if changing my way of thinking would make this more comfortable."

"That's the challenge. The watched well never shrinks."

"This isn't about an unanswered letter, is it?"

"No, it's about an answered one."

We return home. Rosa frisks a Luristan horse's bit for a bit of its past. It is but a flake, a scintilla of the thriller that I am. She puts it aside and gazes at me longingly. It's going to be a sixty-year job at least.

"I've never met any bowl like you," she says, still with little idea of how true that is. She puts her hands ooooooon me.

I give her: one of the most outlandish unions, the couple that spent sixty years insulting each other, without ever repeating an insult. They had considerable wealth so were able to commission fine works of art, sculptures, murals, and literary compositions to revile each other. Their peccadillo made a significant if unrecognized contribution to the history of art in dispensing huge amounts of money to artists. Rosa starts working her way through their collection of traducements and the fantastic wham-bamming occasioned by it.

I want to try more of Rosa's memories. I wheelie in.

2 5

She is carrying a bottle of champagne. She is nervous and annoyed. She presses a bell marked MARK. A face with a garland of blond hair appears at a window above, and then instantly vanishes. It reappears shortly thereafter, knowing it cannot cancel out its previous appearance. There is a smile that is forced, and retrospectively, Rosa has daubed anger over the whole thing.

"You didn't get my message?" Blondie asks.

"No. I waited for an hour, and I came over. I was worried."

"Lettuce called off the supper."

He is shifting from foot to foot. It doesn't take my expertise to see he is agitated. Rosa's perspicacity is hampered because she has come to come. She is in love. She doesn't mind having waited an hour for Blondie; she doesn't mind missing the supper. This is what she was really after anyway.

She undresses until there is nothing left to undress. Such recklessness is untypical of her; it is, of course, not true recklessness, but a long-considered surrender. He is not so great, but she has the power of her imagination.

"What are you doing?" he exclaims, struggling to rebra her breasts.

The abandonment of the act transports her, and she hopes

it will do the same for him. He is shaken by this, and Rosa interprets it as the transmission of lust to all fronts.

"We'll just have to think of something to do," she says.

"There's a great Chinese restaurant around the corner," he suggests.

She chooses to see this as wit and tugs at his track-suit bottom.

"I don't think that's a good idea."

I note a copy of the magazine Tabatha writes for lying on the floor.

Rosa pulls down his covering.

"Rosa, we should get to know each other better."

"No, you can't use that. Men aren't allowed to use that one."

She contemplates the hunched, defensive member, which looks like a midget sulking in a sleeping bag.

"Rosa, I'm really not feeling well."

"This will make you feel better."

But the guest star is reposing. Rosa sticks to his lips and plays tricks on the limp comma, including the yo-yo and the Mexican prisoner, even slapping it around her face, but it is firm in its softness. After ten minutes, its tenderness becomes wounding.

"Don't you find me attractive?"

"You're extremely attractive."

"You were very keen the other week."

"I was. I am. I'm just very tired."

Having spent much of her life enduring the inconveniences of protuberances inflicted on her on dance floors and public transport, Rosa is baffled but decides she has learned an interesting lesson about men and goes to put the champagne bottle in the fridge when Blondie answers the phone. The flat *is sparse—a mattress on the floor, a sofa, and a chair—but there is a massive fridge, the legacy of a big family that must have been squeezed into the flat before. Too late, he spots her going to the fridge.*

She notices that the fridge isn't properly closed and, in a masculine fashion, perishable items are scattered around the kitchen. As she opens the fridge, she discovers a quarter-dressed woman bundled up inside, wearied by hiding there.

"I swear we left a message for you," she says to Rosa, and then adds: "It was only five times." This claim is possibly true since she is clutching that number of condoms and their packaging in her left hand. She is wearing a pair of feather earrings that encode a Swedish journalist using her bottom for purposes of pleasure in Malta, even though the rummaging is far from pleasurable for her because she can't say no.

On the floor on the open page of the magazine Tabatha writes for are members of the alphabet representing the message: If you think your girlfriend's friend is the one for you, the only fair thing is to act.

Rosa's angry, but not only on account of the betrayal; she sees on his face that this was not a switch, but a one-off itch; she sees that Blondie knows he has made a mistake, that Lettuce miragely reflected what he wanted, but now that he has carried out his five-fold investigations he knows it's not there. Rosa knows her fury with Lettuce will pass, but she knows however much she wants to, she can't allow herself to forgive Blondie.

And she isn't even angry with him yet for letting his life be run by a magazine.

Oooooooff come the hands. On goes the night.

Lettuce

The Jehovah's Witness is sitting in the front room, having introduced herself as a friend of Nikki's, or rather as a friend of the girl with dark hair who lives here.

"You're a friend but you don't know her name?"

"Yes," she replied, impervious to the imbecility of her reply. Rosa and her friend Lettuce go to the kitchen.

"I'm worried," says Lettuce. "We didn't use a contraceptive."

Lettuce is wearing the feather earrings suggestive of backdoor Swedish journalism from the fridge incident. Thoughtlessness, I educe, is her chief talent. Her anxiety is not about that liaison; that memory of Rosa's tasted a kidnap-gestating year old.

"Then why did you do it?"

"I wasn't planning to."

"Then why did you go?"

"To talk."

"But you knew his girlfriend was in America."

"Yes, but you know, it was late. We didn't plan to. I had to stay and . . ."

"He confused you with his girlfriend in the dark."

"No. But you know. I hope I'm not . . ."

"Lettuce, what happened the last time you went to see him?"

"You mean when his girlfriend was in Iceland?"

"I can't be sure. It could have been Iceland. Or I might be confusing it with the time she went to Thailand. Or Portugal. I find it hard to keep them in the right order, because every time she's away, you end up going round to see him, doing it all night, and then coming to see me to tell me you're worried about . . ."

103

Lettuce is inspecting the fridge.

"Do you want me to fix you something?"

"No," says Lettuce. "I just want a nibble, if that's okay." She takes out a tub of potato salad and, finding a fork, tucks in with a forlorn air. "I'm not feeling too good."

"At least feel good about it. You're a historian. It's your job to deduce from evidence. You're always telling me people don't learn anything from history. If you're condemned to repeat yourself, at least feel good about it."

"I threw up this morning," she says.

"You're always throwing up. You throw up because you're worried about your exams. You throw up because you're worried about your job. You throw up because you worry about the only long-term relationship you've ever had being with someone who has a girlfriend and whom you sleep with twice a year. You throw up because you're worried about being pregnant. You throw up because you're worried about throwing up."

"I had a long-term relationship with Terry."

"Terry. Yes, that was two months, wasn't it? By your standards, long-term. Mostly conducted thirty to fifty miles outside of London."

"It wasn't his fault the car kept breaking down."

"Well, since it broke down every day for a fortnight I'd say he has to carry some responsibility."

"It wasn't a fortnight. It was only a week. And he wanted to take his kids on holiday, we didn't have the money for the train."

"Or for a car."

"Life's not perfect. Is it better to be as fussy as you are?"

"Well, it's true I'm too finicky to start something with a married man who expects me to look after his three kids for him, to lend him money, and who, after we've spent a couple of weeks on the hard shoulder of a motorway, announces that's it all over because he's gotten someone else pregnant. And let's not forget finding someone in the fridge of the one man whom I was very happy to be with."

"You said we wouldn't talk about that anymore."

"You're right. Sorry."

"Anyway, you didn't miss much, he wasn't that good."

"Lettuce."

"Mind you, he wasn't that bad either."

Lettuce notices she's not going to win this one. She polishes off the potato salad and stares plaintively at the bottom of the tub.

"I could be pregnant," she resumes.

"Well, you could. But if you're worried about being pregnant, and something tells me you are, why not do something to find out whether you are or not?" The coleslaw is removed from the fridge. "I can fix you something to eat if you want." Lettuce shakes her head.

"I'll get a test."

"Good idea. Then we can both get some peace."

"You could be more sympathetic."

"You could be more careful. I was sympathetic the first three times."

"We weren't planning to. Do you have any cheese? You know, I think I'm getting much better at it, but he just does the same things." The cheese and the coleslaw vanish, along with some buns. She struggles with the lid on the jar of pickled beetroot and capitulates. The fruit bowl comes under attack.

"Your mother rang the other day," Rosa announces.

"Again! What did she want?"

"She wanted to know where you are. She probably doesn't believe the story you're in Cambodia."

"You didn't tell her anything? Sainsbury's does better Brie."

"No. I stuck to the story."

"Why won't she leave me alone?"

"She is your mother, and you might consider talking to her once a year, so she doesn't end up interrogating your friends."

"All she does is moan. Every time I talk to her she just complains, about why I don't talk to her, about my father . . ."

"And then she complains about you complaining about her complaining."

"Yes," said Lettuce with a mouthful of apricots, surprised at Rosa's sensitivity to her plight.

"Then you complain about her complaining about you complaining about her complaining. I can't imagine where she gets it from."

"I can leave," says Lettuce, outraged, clutching a yogurt.

"There's someone tapping at the window," reports the Jehovah's Witness.

Rosa goes to the bay window in the front room, which she opens. A figure in a baseball cap is squatting there, evidently, like the Beard, having confused the front of Rosa's abode with a public lavatory. "Got any paper, love?" he inquires. Rosa goes back into the kitchen, fills up the new bucket, and pours it over him. He storms off, threatening to call the police.

"I used to like living here," Rosa muses. "What is going on? Time to sell the flat, I think."

The Jehovah's Witness despairs of waiting for Nikki and goes home.

Close Calls

Rosa takes me out to the cottage. She brings some bedding with her. The countryside has become her home for a few days. She disappears to caress objects, but I am left on a good shelf with plenty of light.

So quiet, I log the passage of dust motes.

The absences are so looooong, I can only educe that Nikki doesn't know my whereabouts, otherwise it would be burglary ahoy.

Rosa returns, dejected and worn. I give her centuries, including the unabridged thirty years of turbot to discourage her from consuming me so ferociously. I give her the lugal whose face went into such funny shapes during the chryselephantine moment (including getting his own tongue into his right ear) that he had to keep executing his concubines for bursting into laughter. Rosa has a chuckle at that.

On the third evening, I am taken out to the well.

"So, verbalize me through it," says Tabatha.

"I thought I'd try the deeply butch stuff. Car-welding for enthusiasts sounded like the sort of course that would attract men, but there were only sixteen other women who looked to me as if they might have had the same idea since they didn't pay much attention to the welding and half of them left early. Even the course tutor was a woman."

"Not to worry. You have to kiss your frogs before you get to the prince."

"But I'm not even kissing frogs."

The Well is getting smarter: "What about your previous relationships?"

"Never mind about those," says Rosa.

We go into the cottage. I am becoming the confidant. Rosa's danger is becoming a tribe of one.

"It's strange—in so many societies, in so many times, it's valued; if I told anyone, they'd laugh, think I was funny in the head. Who knows, perhaps I am?"

She puts her fingers to me. Now, I feel again I'm seeing inside her. Panting memories catch my attention, other memories are crawling out from their chambers.

I leave Rosa with material from the Cruelty Club and backflip into her past.

21

"I'm not going to sleep with you," Rosa says.

"Fine," he says, getting into bed with her.

"Go away," she hisses. She calls for her flatmate, but he is insensibly drunk in the other room, having wassailed the night away.

He turns his back to her. "It's late. I need a place for the night. I'm going to sleep. I'm not going to touch you."

"How stupid do you think I am? If you don't get out, I'll call the police."

"Deal," he says, face deep in pillow.

"Go away," she screams, punching him. He ignores her. She draws up her legs and pushes him out of the bed. He slides to the floor undisturbed, taking the duvet and pillow with him; he curls up with them like a mellow cocoon on a great leaf, unabated in his attempt to slumber. She fumes on the bed. He snores. Three hours later, at four in the morning,

it dawns on Rosa that he is really sleeping and not waiting for drowsiness on her part to have another seduction bid. She begins to nourish a small annoyance that he is not trying to paw her but enjoying such a professional sleep.

"How many women are you sleeping with?" *she asks in the morning after he has eaten her loaf of bread, toasted, with what was left of her marmalade. A twenty-first-birthday card is on the mantelpiece.*

"I don't know," *he says.*

"What do you mean, you don't know?"

"I don't know. I know how many women I'd like to be sleeping with. I know roughly the number of women who've got bits of my gear. But you turn up and sometimes they're pleased to see you, sometimes they're not. Women, you know?" *he says as he carries three tires, an etagère, and a number of Watusi drums into Rosa's room.*

"Do any of them know about the others?"

"Well, Stacey knows about Alex, because Alex is her best friend, but Alex doesn't about Stacey. Sue doesn't know about either Alex or Stacey, or any one of the others, really, but that's the price you pay for living in St. Albans. Jo up in Manchester suspects I'm sleeping with Charlie, which is quite funny because I'm not, but I am visiting Stephanie and Sarah, who work in the same travel agency as her."

His cell phone rings. He makes cooing noises down the phone. "Yeah, yeah, I've just spent the night with a temptress who was gagging for it, but I saved myself for you."

He carries on as he brings in a tribal drum bigger than Rosa: "Then Sophie and Nicole know about each other, because they had a fight over me at the gig in Doncaster. I don't know why—there's plenty of me to go around."

"And you seriously expected me to go to bed with you? You're sleeping with half the nation, and you haven't washed *for quite some time," Rosa retaliates. "Your dress sense was obviously stillborn. And what are you doing bringing all this rubbish in here?" A gong appears.*

"Look, you'll be helping me out."

"Why are you so interested in me?"

"I don't see anyone better-looking here."

She grabs his inner arm and pinches it painfully. He screams.

"Viv and Grace'll vouch for me. You're the one there who hasn't tried me out."

"Do a thorough job, do you?"

"Ask around. Can that many women be wrong?"

Rosa picks up one of the drums. "You don't think this is genuine, do you?"

The drummer stays odd nights. Rosa begins to suspect that he likes the arrangement because no demands are made on his much-in-demand organ. Not in the conventional manner. Ithyphallic, he places sugar cubes on the end of his prong and catapults them across the room while Rosa tries to catch them with her mouth. In a haphazard and intermittent way, they live together for two years, everyone assuming that Rosa was another name on the Drummer's list of clients. She enjoyed seeing that she was the one in the know. The others would phone the Drummer on his cell phone and she would listen with amazement as he brushed them off. She doesn't seek the chryselephantine with him, but she hasn't been fooled by him. She learns a lot about men and women from him.

An unsound sound system is the cause of his death, but I see that attached to this remembrance caravan is her third favorite dream, the one where he walks in, skin defects to the fore; he comes in to collect his Papuan tom-tom and tries to open the jar of pickled beetroot. "Glad you kept this," he says, holding the fraying instrument, "because it's not a tom-tom at all. It's all the decency that's left in the world. Who would think I'd be looking after it?"

Rosa is still engrossed in the Cruelty Club. It is a good one. I ringpull another nearby memory.

"The dog ate the light," he says.
Rosa has a tired-of-supporting-an-ideal-on-her-own evening. Drunk. Drink has pushed her fortifications aside. The bedroom is cold and swaying like a hammock. She sees hints of the chewed lamp from the hallway light as she enters the dark bedroom. Everything about the house is wrong, out of joint, held together by chewing gum. The stairs moan and move.
The ceiling is so low she can barely stand up. The bed is small, saddening, unbeddy. She manages to fall onto it. Under the door she sees a huge wedge of light where the floor and door have gone their separate ways. She takes off the most significant items of clothing . . . the cold and an indifference in her arms stop her going farther. Emmett the ecologist—a name that, once in, can never fall out of anyone's skull—is in the bathroom, freshening his laughing gear. He steps back in a silence that presses into her ears.

She has enough sobriety to feel gratitude for the dark. If she saw him undressed she knows she'd have to change her mind. She laments the strapping ones she sent on their way. Does it have to be so cold, so drumroll-less?

More surprised than lubricious he is, she realizes, like an ailing laboratory mouse, wary of the next prod or indignity. Here we go. She manages to invent the discarding of the bra. She hears a couple of hesitant steps, then a glassy, bottlely sound and a heavy thump. A minuscule "o." After some fumbling, crawling sounds, the light comes back on in the hallway to reveal that Emmett has left a carpet of blood on the floor from his thigh, which has been cut open. His penis, a cedilla in very small print. She tries not to rubbish the rest of his body. He has slipped on one empty bottle of lemonade and fallen on another. This is tedious. Rosa doesn't feel like helping him to a hospital; she's not heartless enough to leave, not heartful enough to care.

Rosa is still going strong in the Cruelty Club. Will she sense that someone has been plucking the fruit of her mind? I cartwheel into an attendant experience.

R o o o o a s o o o

24

On her back, a more-like-it bed. She has debra'd and unknickered; Rosa lies invitingly as possible. His prong is so ridiculously erect, it plugs his navel. He has the confident shanks of a telephone-sales supremo. Smooth chest. Faint six-pack. He appreciates himself for a moment.

Rosa doesn't like him much, but she has to admit, the mood is her master. Telesales looks at Rosa as another mirror in which he can peer at his peerlessness; he administers a couple of anticipatory strokes to the statuette of number one.

The room is de-lighted for delight. Practicedly, Telesales positions himself on the threshold, arched on the starting line; only one traversing thrust to go. Cocked cock. He leaves it there, so their warmths can consult. Perfectly he drops small kisses on her chest. She gives gasps. This was a very good idea. Rosa's left breast is sucked entirely into his mouth; he has recognized its mouthability and takes it for a revolution. A winning scent of soap and musk skewers Rosa. He pulls back slightly. "This may hurt," he says, heralding the pressure.

There is a small "o." Another attempt, another small "o." "Hang on," he says and switches on the light; he stares intently down at himself and raises his hand. It is smeared in blood. As Rosa thinks, That didn't hurt at all, she notices that his prong is ripped and is dripping blood.

Horror conquers every muscle on his face. Concentration lurks, because he doesn't want to do anything sudden or imprudent before he can get it to the best doctors in the world. Cherishing his tool like an expiring messiah, he swathes it in tissues. "Phone for an ambulance," Telesales whispers, afraid that a louder demand might cause further rupture.

Rosa is almost at the end of the Cruelty Club. What a sequence that is. I decide not to probe further into Rosa's past. After all, at this rate, I'll clean her out before she skims my surface.

Trapeze

We return to Rosa's.

Nikki does the pleased-to-see-you routine. She prepares blinis. Afterward, while Rosa is doing the dishes, the buzzer sounds, and Nikki opens the door to a man struggling with an enormous mother-in-law's-tongue.

"Nikki, I've done it. I've left the wife. It's you and me all the way now."

Nikki glowers at this breach of hard fornicating etiquette.

"Darren, let me give you a tip here, which I think you'll find useful. Before you leave your wife and snatch the plant to spend your life with someone new, you should raise the subject with that person first. Otherwise, that person might say, like me: You must be fuhking joking."

Plantman leaves reluctantly. He doesn't listen as well as he carries plants. Nikki betrays too fast to be betrayed.

"Don't you get tired of it all?" Rosa asks.

Nikki shrugs. "Oh, I forgot. What's-her-name, Helen's been looking for you. About the bowl."

Indeed, Marius must be getting impatient.

The next morning Rosa goes out, unusually leaving me behind; as foreseen, Nikki is suddenly very keen to get close to me. Three minutes, forty seconds after Rosa goes off on a date with some belt buckle, I'm onto my three thousand two hundred and eleventh stealing.

"It's hard having a big ego," Nikki reflects, "without having big success. But you ought to help me with that."

No messing around with junk shops now. We go straight to an auction house, the one where I started. Not that Nikki knows that. Nikki tries to see the auctioneeress, but she is out. I hope that she and Rosa will turn up, because I doubt even Nikki's ingenuity would be able to come up with a good line in that situation. We depart.

I get to see Nikki's training ground. She decides to have a good sweat.

The place is dedicated to circus skills of all sorts; to making the smile, the ooooooo. I remember the bull dancers of Crete. The circus has fascinated people for so long. It is not about skills; it is about spreading yarns. That there is happiness. That there is achievement. That there is beauty. That there is resolution, a beginning and an end. It takes place in a ring. There are those who say a circle is a symbol of no beginning and no end; on the contrary it is a symbol showing that the beginning and the end can be anywhere. That is why it is such hard work. They are lighters against the darkness. They have to dispense with problems, crack the whip on misery.

Nikki dangles and climbs for a few hours. She performs the maneuvers known as skinning the cat and the half-angel. Her slender frame conceals great strength, and she is valiant, but next to the eloquence of those who do it for a living, she stutters. There is a smell of cheap coffee and watery tea. She chats with the pros, looks for tips. It thins out and Metaldick struts in.

Nuking ahoy.

Their clothing has a groundbreak; Nikki comes up from behind and twists his nipples like dials; his manhood shoots up like a barrier at a railroad crossing. More construction has taken place since I last observed him; he now inserts into his urethra a thin metal bar which he secures by screwing in a restrainer through one of his piercings. He has basaltness aplenty, so bringing in more hardness is a disinvestment, but this is only the start. He takes another metal object in the shape of a lizard's head and fastens it onto the bar.

They scamper up the ropes. The trapezes and all the gear have been, it seems, pretested so that the arcs are right.

Metaldick's every muscle is conspicuous, not overweening, but they testify to a lifetime of hanging around; no gibbon can teach him a thing. He's got it. You can visualize most of Europe lining up for a munch on his brawn. Still sprightly, Nikki is not as ludicrously hardened as Metaldick; age has made one or two preliminary teases around her body, but her partners won't complain.

They swing sedately toward each other; Nikki's legs pincer around Metaldick's waist and gradually she, with vim and considerable markswomanship, wiggles appropriately and they make a fleshy hammock of themselves.

Holding on like that, there isn't much room to get moving, but with some shuffling and vigorous exhalations and inhalations, they start tapping on pleasure's door. Nikki's suffering becomes quite apparent, her upper body not up to the task. Understandably, with these bumper supplies of fillips she doesn't notice Lump moving in the shadows below.

They have no restrainers, no safety net. They are some twenty feet up, so as a minimum, they could count on some formidable damage to bone or muscle.

Circus types mill around, fashionize on meager budgets. They are not paying too much attention, either because this happens all the time or because it's the custom to act as if it does.

One shaven-headed girl is eating popcorn and telling her friend that she wants to go and visit a friend who is in jail in the South of France; she has a van, although it is in such a bad state she isn't sure it will make it all the way down. She doesn't have any money for gas. She also doesn't have a driver's license, and the police there are apparently funny about things like that. Her friend, a freelance didgeridoo maker, had gone down to the South of France to visit another friend, a nut cutlet consultant, who had ended up in jail because she had gone down to the South of France without a driver's license to visit her when she, Fuzz-head, had been in jail as a result of not having a driver's license when she had gone down to visit a friend, a treehouse architect, who had been in jail because he didn't have a driver's license, though by the time she got down there because the van she had been driving kept on breaking down and running out of gas, he had been released.

Another girl comes in, watches the midair mission. She reaches into her bag and pulls out a camera. There is a flash. Nikki spins out of her ordeal and snarls: "No pictures."

She is so angry and hung up that she doesn't notice Lump deftly lift me from under her windbreaker. Lump fits in here. Everyone thinks she's an act.

We sit in the van patiently, Lump reading the same page (thirteen) of a dictionary over and over. I understand how the invented can fail; how messy news is; how the didactic is too often stuck-up pap. I know the lure of order. An hour and twenty-three minutes later when the incandescent Nikki storms out from the trapeze place, we track her home.

Lump

We go in, Lump having the exact outline for the lock.

Nikki is frozen in the act of packing by the sight of Lump; for the first time since I have known her, she is swatted; a plaything of fear, not able to look for possible exits or weapons.

"Hallo, Nikki."

Nikki is still struggling to appraise the situation. Talk? Beg? Jump out the window?

"I don't suppose you were expecting to see me."

Nikki works up to a no. Her knees are about to give way.

"No, I don't suppose I'd be expecting to see someone I'd shot six times in the chest either."

This is said with calm reflection, like a schoolgirl working out if twelve earthworms go to a disco in Bogotá at nine o'clock, how long is it before they get stepped on? It is not simulated coolness, a chill preamble to a flaring rage; it is deluxe dispassion.

Nikki concluded she is not about to die in the coming seconds, and even if she is, deprived of sharp objects, decisive weaponry, there's not much she can do since the normally trusty shooting-Lump-six-times didn't do the job.

"Not to mention the shot in the head," Lump adds. Her face shows no mark, but this is perhaps the origin of her two gold teeth.

"You're looking well," says Nikki. "Cup of tea?" Neat maneuver: friendliness and moving closer to the knives in the kitchen in one go. She is back on the case.

118

Nikki moves to the kitchen, noting that I have been returned.

"So it was you that brought the stuff back, was it?"

"Yes."

"I'd never have worked it out. I'm not sure the wings are really you."

"I've come to bring you a message."

"A message?"

"A message from the other side. I had to die to bring it to you."

"Die?"

"You killed me. I was dead. Six bullets in the chest, not to mention the one in the head."

Nikki switches on the kettle. "For what it's worth, I'm sorry. The gun just went off, and when I saw you'd been hit . . . I was scared you'd, you know, pull me apart. I just panicked and kept on going. Next thing I knew . . . it was empty."

"I can't blame you. And I'm sure you've forgiven yourself for it. I did have a terrible temper. You were right to do it."

"I wouldn't say that."

"You were right to do it, because it changed both our lives."

"So what happened? They fixed you up at the hospital? Sorry I didn't call an ambulance, but I didn't think you'd be needing one."

"They didn't fix me up. I was pronounced dead. Then I changed my mind."

"How did you do that?"

"One of the mortuary attendants persuaded me to return."

"Pardon?"

"Menstuff. . . . The perverse are not above doing good. I'm surprised you didn't hear about my recovery. Big news."

"I was gone. I was gone before you hit the floor. I guess by the time you got to the hospital, I was at the airport."

"Have you been abroad all this time, then?"

"Yeah," says Nikki, "mostly. So what's the message?"

"The message is you can't go on living your life like this."

"You came all the way from heaven to tell me that? A postcard would have been easier."

Nikki has rocketed from malodorous terror to cheek in under a minute. She knows she is safe. I hesitate whether to place her at number one hundred and thirty-two or number one hundred and thirty-three in my list of people readers.

"I thought a lot when I was in hospital. I hadn't led a particularly bad life. Beat the shit out of a few people, but that was my job. They were mostly asking for it. I did some wilder things when I was younger. I used to go into pubs and say to the beer-drinking slobs: 'Do you fancy my girlfriend?' If they said yes, I'd thump 'em; if they said no, I'd say, 'Why not?' and thump 'em."

"What if they said they'd have to think about it?"

"No one said that. I used to dislike them because I thought they had it easy."

It is true; the worst thing is to be spiritually bed-sitted, to believe the well you're down is deeper than everyone else's.

"Do you ever play computer games?" asks Lump.

"Sometimes."

"They're the clues. The more sophisticated ones have different levels of difficulty. You can choose different tactics. You pick up various tools. Trowels. Nukes. Aardvarks. Whatever. You and I, you and I and everyone else—we're in a game."

"But we don't get to choose our level of difficulty."

"We don't remember it. Part of the game. Most things that are worthwhile are difficult."

"Plenty of difficult things aren't worthwhile, just difficult."

"When I was in hospital, it was far from certain that I would survive. I didn't feel I should have had more money, had more sex; I did feel that I should have done more good."

"So, how should I change my life?"

"No more theft, no more hurt, no more unpaid bills, no more shootings, no more deaths."

"What about muff diving?" catechizes Nikki. She moves forward to Lump. "Come on, show me your scars." She undoes Lump's front, while the woman sits impassively. She takes Lump's two immense breasts, each the size of a guard dog, pulls them together so that one tongue can lick two nipples. Nikki has switched herself on like a scortatory bonfire, but after eighty seconds of blowing out *oooooos* she stops, because Nikki knows this is doing as much for Lump as if she were nibbling the windowsill in the other room.

"I have a word for you. *Anhedonia.* I am beyond pleasure."

"Anne Hedonia. That'd make a good alias for me. You definitely died, there's no doubt about that."

"Believe me, these worldly things, they fall to your feet like dirty clothes that don't matter. Your whole self falls off like a false nail on the floor."

How come no one asks the false nail how it feels?

"So you believe this good-and-evil ticket?"

Indeed, the popularity of good and evil, that dynamic duo, has baffled me. Things have always struck me as a struggle between evil and evil. On a good day. A struggle between evil and evil and evil is common. A struggle between evil and evil and evil and evil is not unknown. I have indubitably witnessed struggles between evil and evil and evil and evil and evil and evil and evil.

"I am telling you. You must change. I took a vow when I was in the hospital that I would do something to change the world; that means you."

She looks placidly at Nikki, who thinks about this.

"How can you take it seriously?" she says. "All that stuff about diet? One man's steak is another man's god."

"All I know is what I feel."

"So you're going to keep an eye on me."

"Yes. You should choose, but if you choose badly, I'll be around to give you a chance to choose again."

"Yeah?" Nikki has bolted from terror to the outskirts of boredom; now she is wondering if any benefit can be extracted from Lump.

"How many friends do you have? Is there anyone from your past who would like to see you? And if there is, isn't it because they want to break your neck?"

"How's Stinky?"

"Okay. His business went bust."

"I'm surprised. He's such an arsehole, you'd have thought he couldn't fail."

"What about you? What do you have to show for it? Underwear with holes?"

"It's true I haven't got a spiffy pair of wings like that. I move around a lot. I made a wish on my fourteenth birthday, in Market Harborough, that I didn't mind what happened to me: slavery, eaten by sharks, gunned down in a backstreet of a dingy city, starve, or whatever, I didn't mind how brutal or even unpleasant it was, as long as I was as far away as possible from Market Harborough, in the last place on earth I could imagine. I wanted something beyond imagination."

"We are all our own executioners."

"Eh?"

"It was my choice to fall for you. Who else can I blame but myself?"

"Right."

"I can see I haven't made much of an impression on you. Just ask yourself why you need it all, the needle and the bodies."

"Let me see. Because it's bloody good fun?"

"We both know you're lying."

"I got a globe when I was a kid. I used to play with it, if you know what I mean. I didn't really know what I was doing but it was fun. Could be why I've always wanted to have the world between my legs. I stuck a knitting needle through it eventually, to find the place on the other side of the world, farthest away. It was never the same. That's what matters— to be on the road, to be the one, the girl wrapped in boys."

Objects are always coming in for it, objects are always being treated like objects; I have been subjected to indignities you wouldn't believe a ceramic could face, but we, too, are tied down on the paths of libido. Mostly men who are always seeking to bury their prongs into something—keyholes, arm-chairs, watermelons, pademelons, but women, too, have seen us as emissaries that can intercede with the merchants of pleasure.

"So, what did you tell the police?" asks Nikki.

"I kept you out of it." Lump avers, "there's less for one of your aliases to worry about. I gave them a description of a freakishly large woman, short hair, early thirties. They didn't seem to catch on that I was giving them my own description. But I was responsible. I was obsessed with you, and if you hadn't been so scared of me you wouldn't have started shooting. You have to understand responsibility."

"Oh, yeah," says Nikki, pouring the tea.

123

"Don't you see what you have done is wrong and is making you unhappy?"

"If this is unhappiness, I can cope. There are two sorts of people, the betrayers and the betrayed. There's one easy way of avoiding being betrayed."

"When you're alive, you always worry about not having had enough. Why did I only take forty pounds from the till and not a hundred? Why didn't I punch Stinky? Why did I punch Phil? Why didn't I kick him in the head as well? Why didn't I ask for more? Why didn't I take more?

"When you're dead it's different. You think, Why didn't I lend Alma the money when she needed it? Why didn't I lend Sophie more? Why did I cheat on her? Why did I make both of us miserable for an extra lick or two?

"You have to see what's important. There was a guy in a pile-up I tried to help, he was trapped in a metal straitjacket and was bleeding to death. There was nothing anyone could have done. He didn't call for poetry or money or a beautiful painting to contemplate or want to make an announcement to the press. He only wanted to hold a hand, and even a complete stranger's would do. I know what I'm talking about."

"So you're here to make me happy?" Nikki inquires. Lump nods.

"How about fuhking off, then?"

"I'll leave. I've delivered the message. But, Nikki, do understand I'm not leaving because you asked. Making you happy doesn't mean doing what you want. Don't forget, I know you quite well."

Lump moves to the door. She counts out some money. "If you really need some, let me give you some. And I found you. Don't forget that. I'd be surprised if I were the only person looking for you.

"Oh. One more thing. It was good of you to shoot me."

"Don't mention it."

Lump leaves. The price of vegetables could have been the subject of the conversation. I educe that she and Nikki lived together for several months some three years ago; the specific cause of Nikki ventilating Lump remains a mystery, but there is no doubt that it will happily fit into the category of doing something you massively shouldn't be doing.

Strangerness has settled on them. The only hint of their one-time (three-times-a-night) intimacy comes from the shooting. Their nuking has left no fallout. No evidence. It is the perfect crime. People lose everything: their earrings, their teeth, their hopes, their outrage, their intimates, their memories, and themselves; the one thing they can't lose is loss. The loss of loss. Ending ending. That's the big project. Ask a collector.

While love can evaporate depositlessly, you rarely forget someone you've shot. Ask an old soldier.

Well Well

Rosa reclaims me. If she'd have returned home ten minutes later, I have no doubt I would have been on a new stealing number.

We go out to the countryside. Go to the well. No burbling. Rosa shines a torch down in case Tabatha has shrunk and adopted a vicious taciturnity. Zero.

Gone. Rosa's not good at this game.

She's worried about what might have happened to Tabatha and, inevitably, quite worried about the consequences. Nikki would find this twist amusing. We home in on home.

In a new chair, Rosa tries to read a newspaper article

about two AIDS specialists who had a one-night stand at a World AIDS Congress. They are suing each other, since both claim the other one gave them AIDS.

Nikki arrives: "You look miserable."

"Hard day at the authentication. I'm so miserable I don't even feel like shopping."

"There is no lower point."

Tabatha is all over Rosa's thoughts. A decision approaches. She rises. Prognostication: She is going to look for her.

"I'll be out for a while if anyone's looking for me." Nikki smiles helpfully as Rosa leaves.

Without me? A Nikki nicking?

Wordless, Reparteeless

Nikki goes to her room to consider packing; then she goes to the bathroom and starts running a final bath.

They enter stealthily as a smell; they must have investigated the lock earlier. They have waited for Rosa to leave.

Their clothes are carefully chosen, cheap-popular trainers, cheap-popular jeans, cheap-popular blousons, cheap-popular baseball caps, roomy so you would have a hard time saying anything definite about their build. They are so nondescript as to be invisible. Only now, presumably, have they donned the balaclavas to make their faces those of cheap-popular killers. Gloves. Cropped heads. Yompers.

Type forty-one killers: They'll go home and clean the oven. They look the same everywhere, that's what's funny, with or without the knitting. No fuss, almost yawning, they do this for a living.

Nikki is in the bathroom, listening to music. Wordless

(One Hundred Sixty-Five) carries a bag, which he now opens. Reparteeless (Ninety-Five) produces a small handgun with a silencer and checks the rest of the flat for occupancy, draws the curtains.

Wordless has produced a video camera and a small chain saw from the bag. They nod to commence the assignment.

Then Rosa walks back in, presumably because she wants me or has forgotten something else.

Nikki comes out of the bathroom, and everyone meets at the same time. Wordless and Reparteeless gesture that the two should lie on the ground.

"The bowl's over there," says Rosa.

Their incurable lack of interest is plain.

"Oh, God," says Rosa. "Tabatha's sent you, hasn't she?"

"It's nothing to do with you," says Nikki. Wordless indicates that she should strip. She takes off her top. She has no problems with letting her body get in the running. Wordless indicates more. "All of it?" she asks. He nods. She doesn't mind this bit.

"Is it Shiner?" she asks. No response.

"Is it Phil?" No response.

"The Cash Brothers, then?"

Wordless starts to tie her hands to the table legs.

"Oh, God," Nikki says, having worked out by elimination who's behind this. Now she'd given herself to worry.

"I'll offer you twice what you're being paid." Wordless rubs finger and thumb in inquiry.

"I haven't got it here, but . . ." Wordless has already turned up the music and warmed up the chain saw.

"Why don't you let me do some things for you, a bit of pleasure before business?" Nikki offers, a tone of fear in her voice no one has ever heard. Reparteeless sets up the video camera and speechlessly indicates that there's something wrong with it. Despite the balaclava and mutism, Wordless is furious about this.

Then the door flies halfway across the hallway as if competing in the long jump. Wordless and Reparteeless look at each other.

"This is too much," says Wordless, feeling he is in a universe where professionalism is derided and punished. White-winged Lump is standing before them, not looking any smaller than usual.

"Good-bye, gentlemen," she says in a tone so unthreatening it seems insane in the circumstances. Wordless slips. He has the gun, but instead of doing the job, he tries to be funny. He casually shoots Lump in the leg, expecting her to collapse in agony. Perhaps if he had smashed the knee, he would have had some satisfaction, but he merely punctures her ample thigh, leaving a crimson scallop on the wall behind. Instead of folding, Lump grabs his hand and rotates it somewhere between 450 and 452 degrees, not paying any attention to the snapping sounds.

Prognostication: face-defacing.

Within the same second she slams a blackness-bringing fist into the balaclava. One moment he has a face, the next he doesn't. Limp as a wet cloth. "I have a word for you," she says but Wordless is witless, not in the market for vocabulary extensions. *"Analgesia."*

Reparteeless has the chain saw. The smart money would have been on him going in with it, because in this sort of altercation, it's hard to top a chain saw. However, he views the chain saw as unsporting, or he wants to get something out of the money he has spent on martial arts classes; he goes in with a roundhouse kick to the face, which, if it works, is unique in its efficacy. But the trouble with such a maneuver is

128

that it needs one hundred percent application, a ninety-nine percent successful kick is no good. Lump grabs and halts the foot six inches from her face. The trouble with street fighting, like war, is that there's no reward for second place.

"This is for being flashy," she says, twisting the foot so violently you can hardly hear the ligaments and bone go.

Prognostication: firmest knee to the groin.

"And you know what this is for," she says, grabbing him by his testicles and propelling him up and up, shooting his head through the ceiling, a move, I must admit I've never seen before. I applaud as I am able. She releases him, the body flopping, Reparteeless's consciousness having left the body to its own devices.

"Pity the camera wasn't working," remarks Nikki, not as composed as her words would suggest. "I wouldn't mind being untied." Lump undoes the ropes while Rosa attempts to comes to terms with two hired killers bursting into her home, coming within a hair of extinguishing her, and seeing them binned.

"Thank you," says Nikki uncharacteristically, resuming clothing. "How did you know?"

Lump smiles. Nikki is unsettled by this. She is beginning to credit Lump with supernatural powers, but she should really credit her with fitting a listening device when she returned the objects. Wordless groans softly; Nikki kicks him sharply in the stomach.

"I'll phone the police," says Lump. "I think they will find it pleasurable talking to our friends."

"The police?" Nikki queries. Horror. Revulsion. You must be joking.

"Do you have a better idea?" Patiently. Nikki does have some ideas but sees that they won't make her life any better. She settles for sporadically kicking the distressed groaners until the police arrive and she lapses into her wounded flower routine.

"Doesn't that hurt?" Rosa asks Lump.

"No."

Rosa can't digest this. "I had a mouse in the kitchen once."

Cup of Tea: Twenty

They return from the police station after much exchanging of information. I have been guarded without any enthusiasm by junior members of the Metropolitan Police. The door has been persuaded to resume something like its original duties.

"I suppose the only thing left now is for the house to be burned down," says Rosa.

"I'm sorry," says Nikki, and this is almost true. "I'll go if you want."

"No. Why? What else can possibly happen? I actually feel quite up. By the law of averages, I must have had my lifetime's supply of bad luck. The only way is up." Above, musical sounds trickle down from the head-sized hole.

The tea is made.

"I still don't completely understand why your friend Lump was parked outside," Rosa comments.

"I'm not sure I do," Nikki reflects. "You can love them, but sometimes they can't leave you."

"So who's Shiner?" asks Rosa. "And the what Brothers?"

"Who's Tabatha?"

"Uh—"

"Shiner's . . . never mind. I know who was behind this. Lal, a brother of one of my former clients. Can't remember his name now; he wasn't very memorable, as a person. As a discipline client, he was one of the better ones."

"Is there much difference?"

"Oh, yeah. Some can be awful. I had this card done: DOMI-NATION. 'Cause I thought it'd be easier, more fool me. First client I had was this huge Scots navvy, who gets off his gear and says, 'Hurt me,' so I get out the cat-o'-nine-tails and give him a playful flick, and he turns around and belts me in the mouth. 'That hurt, you bitch,' he says. I thought my jaw was broken. But you know, in some ways domination can be a pushover at first. You get this Asian travel agent crawling around, licking your stilettos, and saying: 'Punish me, mistress, I am dirt. By the way I can get you a great deal to Karachi.' So you get him to vacuum the room, clean the windows, polish your shoes, but you know, there are only so many household tasks. I had them doing the neighbors' gardens after a while. Doing the neighbors' toilets. Doing their shopping. Never does any harm to be on good terms with your neighbors. Then I'd get one to make some mess, shit on some dishes, and the next one to clean it up. But it's, you know, a pain. They expect you to be always hovering around, giving out some lash or abuse, you couldn't go off down to the pub, or watch television, and it's not as if they do the job properly. I told one to clean the bathroom, and he just couldn't; I got really annoyed with that one. I gave him such a good thrashing he tipped me fifty.

"But like anything else, you get the hang of it; after a while I weeded out the stroppy ones and I came up with the idea of the dungeon. Wasn't a dungeon really, it was just a large truck with a few modifications, but I'd stick them in the *dungeon*, so then I could get some peace and quiet. And it made everyone very happy, 'cause I'd leave them there for a day or so, I gave them a cheap rate, a bit extra if they wanted me to look in once in a while and answer their prayers by pissing on them.

131

"So, anyway, one of my best clients was Lal's brother. He worked for the Electricity Board, as a clerk, so he earned nothing, but he worked in the accounts department. I had this huge unpaid bill, I think I hadn't paid it for a year. They'd been coming around, trying to disconnect me for months, they were just about to dig up the road to cut me off, when he cancelled the bill. So for a fee, I'd also arrange for my neighbors to have no electricity bills, and by the end it was the whole street and most of the next block, all the local restaurants and businesses. I don't think I've ever been so popular, and this herbert would have his weekends in the dungeon.

"One weekend I have this electrical man in the dungeon and another dungeon running with some guy from Lambeth council. It's Sunday afternoon, a nice hot summer's day. They've been in the dungeons since Friday night, no food or drink, just harsh language, a reek's coming from the boxes, and I'm just about to let them out. I've done all the house-work, done me exercises, I'm feeling pleased with myself, been a good girl, so I think I'll give myself a treat. I decide just to nip out to my friendly next-door dealer.

"This dealer's a terrible arsehole. Dr. Delight—if you looked up the word *loser* in an illustrated dictionary, it'd have his picture. I never knew what his real name was, 'cause he actually changed it legally, but I'll bet you it's one of the five most boring names in history. But he's five minutes' walk away, so I go out in the sunshine for a little stroll. I get to Delight's, score, and I'm about to leave when he gets terribly friendly, offers me some vodka, new works, suggests I shoot up. So I think, why not? Delight has to bribe people to talk to him. The lads'll be grateful for another half an hour in the slammer. I have a drink, put the metal to the flesh. I'm feeling good, too good. Unbelievably, what I've actually suc-

132

ceeded in doing is buying drugs from a drug dealer. The stuff I've shot is real; it's not the traditional rubbish that's been cut. The last thing I remember is Delight offering me some snake for supper and him looking a bit worried. Then I'm gone, gone, gone.

"I'd suspect him of doing it deliberately, except he's too much of fuck. Just a quality-control slip. What happened next I pieced together later. So I flake out with that hard-to-imitate about-to-die look. Delight freaks, of course. He flushes his stash down the loo, but fair's fair, he phones for an ambulance. So there we are, me out, ambulance on the way. Delight sweating it and thinking up a good story to cover the events. Course it's summer and I'm not wearing too much. Delight starts to think, the ambulance might be a while and I was in no position to say no to a quick florida.

"So, he's on the job, trousers at half-mast, when his girl-friend walks in. I should say, Delight collects all sorts of odd items. His flat's like an antique shop—well, a really shitty one. There's a diver's suit, stuffed cassowary—"

"Cassowary?"

"Stuffed cassowary. It's like an ostrich. I'm sure he got it because everyone would think it's an ostrich and say, Why've you got a stuffed ostrich? So he could say, no, no, it's a *cassowary*. Another opportunity to look interesting. I don't know where he got his money from, 'cause it couldn't have been from dealing or anything that depended on effort on his part. No chance. But he had all sorts of stuff stuffed, expensive. You know, if someone else told you something like that, you might think 'that's interesting, I didn't know that,' but with Delight you just think, 'You boring sod, you're trying to make me think you're interesting.' He also had a thing about medieval weapons.

"So his girlfriend fires a crossbow into his arse and then

hits him over the head with an abacus. He's out for the count. She's not too bright, or maybe she sees the vodka and thinks I'm drunk or I just like sleeping on Delight's floor with no knickers. She goes through my bag, finds the rest of the smack. She shoots up with it, and a couple of seconds later flops over Delight, conked out.

"Then two other dealers come in. The other dealers in the area only let Delight stay in business 'cause they like to amuse themselves by beating him up and taxing him regularly. What happens next is rather murky. The two of them start to argue, whether it's because they can't find Delight's stash or whether it's over the money they've eased from Delight's pockets, or whether they can't make up their mind as to who should have first go with me still in an accommodating pose; they start to fight. I think it might have been over the stash, 'cause one of the dealers gets battered senseless with—wait for this—a frozen iguana that Delight had in the freezer, 'cause of fancying himself as a taxidermist. There were these gerbils everywhere that looked as if they'd been in serious road accidents 'cause Delight couldn't get it right. Apparently the iguana's quite a tasty little tool, as by this point there's blood all over the flat. Though the dealer who goes down fights back with Delight's half-doped cheetah."

"Half-doped cheetah?"

"Yeah. Half-doped cheetah. I hadn't seen it 'cause it was in another room, but Delight apparently had this cheetah—this is a council flat mind you, on the twelfth floor; again no doubt to help with his problem of not being very interesting. Somehow he'd given it some smack—presumably so he could go down the pub and say 'My cheetah's got a terrible habit'—so the cheetah was well out of it, until it found itself being swung round by its tail.

"Then the first of the ambulance men come in. He slips on

134

the blood on the floor, bangs his head, is out cold. The second ambulance man comes in and is clobbered by the afore-mentioned iguana, still going strong, presumably because the dealer thinks he's another dealer in disguise come to tax Delight, since Delight has, having been beaten up several times, become very fussy about opening the door. Or maybe he's just trying to get out, since he's so keen to leave that he rushes out, sprints into the street, and gets run over by a bus.

"So, two days later, I come to in the hospital. The first thing I see is a nurse, with a line of policemen behind her, who hands me an award. 'It's from the hospital staff, they present this every year to the most outlandish admission of the year.' It normally goes to someone with an otter trap up his arse or his dick down a vacuum cleaner, but although it's only August, they feel sure I'm going to walk away with it, an overdose being a bit pedestrian, but they felt my interpreta-tion was something special.

"Then I realize I've been out for two days. The two hottest days of the year, as it turns out. After a while, I think about the dungeons. I sneak out of the hospital in none too good condition and get back to the flat. One of the dungeons has moved right across to the other side of the room; it's our elec-trician, who obviously was struggling furiously trying to get out. He's gone, I discover, to cringe before the great thigh-booted dominatrix in the sky. The Lambeth council worker, perhaps 'cause he's used to lying around, doing nothing, is comatose but still breathing."

"He was lucky."

"Yeah, but it also might have been because I gave him a drop just before I had gone out to Delight's. 'What a weekend' was all he said before I rushed off to the airport. I didn't feel too good about it, obviously, but you pays your money, you take your chance. I'd always wanted to go to

135

America. Anyway, the trouble was the Electrician's brother, this Lal, who's famous for his lack of sense of humor. The Electrician would get mugged by a couple of seven-year-olds, his brother spends his leisure time cutting open security vans. I don't think Lal was close to his brother but he doesn't like to go into pubs and think people might be whispering, Yeah, his brother died in a tart's box."

"And what was the other name you mentioned. Shiner?"

"Don't even ask. That was America. Just don't ask."

"You should write a book."

"Who'd fuhking believe me?"

Cup of Tea: Twenty-Nine

The buzzer goes. Nikki: out trapezing. Rosa: in, all worked up. It is Tabatha. Inured to outrageous surprises, Rosa admits her as if she had been expected.

"I'm surprised you didn't just call the police," says Rosa.

"It did cross my mind. What happened to your door? Milk, no sugar, thank you."

"How did you get out?"

"I'd tried climbing out by pressing my back and legs against the well and sort of shuffling up, but I was too soft in the tummy department to do it at first, but I had a go every day and generally there was improvement."

"Every day in every way you got better and better?"

"Yes and no. And it didn't do my dress any good. But finally I made it to the top, and if there had been a phone in the cottage, I think I would have had recourse to the boys in blue, but by the time I got to a phone, I'd calmed down a little. I realized that I'd lost a lot of weight while I was down there and I started to see that you must have felt quite

136

strongly to have stuffed me down a well. And I could see that, in a way, you were right, what good is my profession if I can't apply it successfully to one specific case? After all it's not your fault you had this idea to kidnap me."

Tabatha is wearing a pair of agate earrings betokening a crotchety old man grumbling about his pub—where the beer is disgusting and watered down and where everyone hates him—changing its name. She doesn't know this, nor does she sense it.

"Wasn't anyone looking for you?"

"No. It's rather irritating. You think you're going off to teach a seminar and you're down the bottom of a well for two weeks; you get back to find a few bills and a few polite inquiries on your answering machine about your copy. Even the plants seem to have fared quite well. Everybody simply assumed I was busy or I had sneaked off for a holiday."

"I have the word *failure* branded on my soul," says Rosa.

"That would be a good trick. Listen, I'm going to invite you to a party. We're going to fix you up. It's rather ridiculous, a good-looking girl like you being on her own." Tabatha picks up the jar of pickled beetroot and tries to twist the lid.

"I could get a date in five minutes. I just have to walk out the front door and flag down the nearest male. It's getting someone who doesn't walk on all fours."

"When in doubt, throw a party. We'll get the men to come by telling them there are too many women, and we'll invite lots of people we don't know. That always works."

"Why am I this way?" wonders Rosa. "Why can't I just be a whore?"

They have another cup of tea.

"Trust me," assures Tabatha. "What's the point of us being here if we can't help each other?" She makes short work of the pecan pie. Rosa escorts her to the door. Outside, a man in a baseball cap is urinating lengthily. He shakes and then produces a knife to rob Tabatha.

"I understand your anger," says Tabatha. "But I can't give you my money because that would make you a criminal and I wouldn't want you harming your future prospects on my conscience."

He snatches her purse.

"I warn you," says Tabatha. "I have an excellent memory and I'm prepared to use it. If you don't return my bag this instant, I shall provide the police with a first-rate description."

The Cap saunters off, belching and rummaging through the handbag, ejecting compacts and lipsticks.

"Just look at what we've done," says Tabatha.

Vote Now

"I don't know why people want to be rich. Why people go on about money is beyond me," says Marius, giving Rosa a warm smile as if he's still hoping she'll think of him as a favorite uncle.

"Child murderers. Child murderers. They have people to help them, they have people who feel sorry for them. The scum that lie in the streets, they have hordes of people to tend to them, to listen to them, to worry about them. They get sympathy. But if you are rich, if you are doing things that benefit people, if you have companies that help people improve their lives, everyone hates you. They spend all their nights thinking up ways to take your money or kidnap you or your family. And it's such a nuisance keeping an eye on the money."

"Give me a couple of million then, Marius," says Rosa,

watching him with the contempt reserved for wildly loath-
some carbuncles.

"I wouldn't do that to you," says Marius, presuming that
the concern he is showing might give him another crack at
Rosa. "It's such a nuisance. Do you know how many banks,
large banks, with intelligent people, intelligent, educated
people running them in safe countries without wars, just go
bankrupt? Just disappear overnight, poof, like a fart? With
millions of hopes. What can you do? I've even bought some
mountains. You think, at least, nothing is going to happen to
a mountain, no one can steal a mountain."

"Well, someone might if they were persistent. A bit of
gravel every day," says Rosa. Marius worries about this for a
sliver of a second, before continuing:

"And you may joke, but even mountains can crumble.
And you talk to one expert who says the mountain's as safe as
houses. You talk to another who says maybe this mountain's
not that safe. So you get a third expert who says yes, it is safe
for the moment, but who knows how long that will be? I
could do another study for another fee. It's terrible, a mountain in Indonesia just fell apart the other week. What can you
trust?"

Marius has come for me.

He doesn't know I'm hidden under the sideboard. Rosa
has told him that I've been given back to the custody of the
auctioneeress, and she, conveniently, as Rosa knows, is away
on holiday for two weeks in an unobtainable style. Which is
doubly convenient for Rosa, since the auctioneeress, too, has
been asking for me. Rosa is finding it impossible to invent
excuses for keeping me.

Marius talks a lot. Possibly he is waiting for Nikki to come
home so he can slime all over her. Perhaps he just stays
everywhere, gibbering until he is thrown out. Rosa should

start coughing on him or activate his fire extinguisher. He gives an awful grimace, like a piano keyboard that's been thrown off a cliff.

"Everyone hates you. The people you've sued. The people you're using. The people you haven't sued. The people who haven't been born yet, they already hate you before they exist. There are millions, hundreds of millions people out there already who aren't out there but who will be because the poor who can least afford it are the keenest to have children, and they hate you. It's a frightening responsibility, money. At least I can console myself that my suffering might help make people happier."

Perhaps it is true; everyone does get what they deserve in the end.

I fear that Marius is whizzing unstoppably toward number-one arsehole of all time. He does have some stiff competition.

My vote goes to the Boetian, Agathon, who lived in a peace-loving community, which was securely poor since, being peace-loving, everyone for hundreds of miles would come over to take anything they fancied and to put the boot in; eventually when the community got poor enough, the visitors dried up. Being peace-loving, they enjoyed austerity since they felt it was bracing. They weren't much good at spreading the doctrine, since by the time they got as far as— "We believe in peace because . . ."—they had usually been punched in the mouth by their addressee, who would then stop any more discourse by giving them a good going-over. Agathon was always wandering around, saying things like, "But why's peace so great, then?" In any other society, they would have pulverized him or put him in a bag with rocks for company and tossed him into the sea. But they were peace-loving and believed in discussion. They discussed. "Yeah, but why's peace so great, then?" Agathon would continue, "Could I have some of your beans, then?" "Could I have the plot of land at the top of the hill?" Then he would say, "Could I have the plot of land at the bottom?" Then, "Could I have the plot of land in the middle?" When they gave him the plot in the middle, he would say, after a few weeks, "Why did you give me this plot? It's useless."

"But you asked for it."

"You shouldn't have listened to me."

They tried avoiding him. They stayed up all night. So did Agathon. They tried hiding at one end of the village. Agathon found them. He never slept and he always asked the most annoying questions: "Do you know that you've got a huge pimple on the end of your nose?" "Did you know you have no teeth left at all?"

Peacefully, they fought back.

"We've had a meeting, Agathon, and we've voted that you're no longer allowed to ask the question 'What's so great about peace?' anymore."

"Okay, but what's so great about voting?"

"We've taken a vote, Agathon."

"But my beans didn't vote."

"Beans aren't allowed to vote, Agathon."

"Why not?"

"All right, beans are allowed to vote. Our beans vote against yours."

"No, they don't. You're putting words in their mouths."

Finally, one night the whole community stole away to a new location. They rested, and when they awoke, they found Agathon there: "I don't think we voted on moving, did we?"

They started telling stories of a fabulous village many hundreds of miles farther down the coast where all those called Agathon would be feasted and entertained by the most beautiful women in the world. He didn't budge. They stole away in the middle of the afternoon, in the greatest heat, when Agathon was asleep, striding off in separate directions and congregating again after convoluted hiking. There were ten people who arrived after Agathon: "Did we vote on this one?"

They traveled up and down the coast and back again. Finally after having suffered decades of privation, split lips, fractured skulls, ruptured stomachs, and people micturating on them at their leisure, they decided they had to rub out Agathon. "It means abandoning our principles," one said.

"No, no, no. It just means putting them down for a second or two. We can draw lots for who should do it."

I don't know whether they did or not because I, as an ovoid loutrophos, the sole remaining possession of the group, I was snatched by a passing Lacedemonian, who gave my holder a powerful punch in his left ear, which annoyed him because he had been seeking to be punched in the mouth since he had a niggling toothache.

"Money," says Marius, "can't buy you the things you really want. When I was a child, we had nothing. I didn't know it at the time. You assume what you have is what you get. I thought everyone didn't have much to eat and was cold. It is only now when I look back at that freezing, dark room I was in with my mother that I can see what it was. No matter how hard you eat, you can't get food back to the years of famine. Nothing can change that.

"I starved as a child because I had nothing, and now in my old age, I have to starve myself because I have everything and I'm fat."

Rosa, quite rightly, snorts at the idea of Marius dieting; his idea of self-restraint would be snubbing the fourth helping of dessert. Feint. Just as you can smear excrement on a gold ingot, so you can drop a speck of gold dust on a turd. Natures are natures.

Marius gets panicky; he fears that his staff might be stealing his mansion and leaves. "You can get a lot of money for bricks. You wouldn't believe it."

Rosa comes to me.

As she puts her hands on me, I decide to show her the roughhouse of loooooove.

The Telescoper of San Francisco

He loved sparkling white wine, not champagne. "Every time you drink champagne, you give money to a Frenchman."

He loved it best decanted through young women; they didn't have to be slim, or big-breasted, or blond, or tall. He was catholic like that. "Aren't you ashamed?" one asked. "Life, like me, like all the best things, is short," he retorted.

He had a book with the addresses of all the women he had slept with—not by the standards of sexual athletes, a large number—and the addresses and details of many women he hadn't bedded but had courted. He sent them cards for every birthday and the anniversaries of their meeting, and small but pleasing presents, presents that were all about reflection on and observation of the recipient's tastes, carefully tailored earrings, magnificent chocolates, rare perfumes. He was always ready to make a purchase and would often buy an item eight months in advance of giving, merely to make sure his gift was unmatchable.

He could not bear to forget or to be forgotten. "We need military precision. We are fighting a war against oblivion. Every time someone forgets you, a part of you dies."

He couldn't stop being kind to women; nothing darkened his face like a letter returned because the address had changed or because a woman was annoyed with him. He couldn't stop buying them flowers and taking off their clothes, making a note of their birthdays, their favorite colors, their favorite music. While he made love to women, he would say, "You are the most beautiful woman who has ever lived," and he would mean it.

Nevertheless, he had been divorced three times. He hated it when a wife would walk in and say, "You've ruined my life."

After the third he decided to lock his heart away because he could only love one way; and it was not to spare himself, but because he couldn't bear feminine unhappiness. He had a mild mania for ceramics: He had a resplendent spherical aryballos with unbelievably brilliant hatching and a vase with a Gorgon design that was unaccountably found one day smashed into two hundred and thirty-six pieces.

One night, staring out the window at the darkness no smaller than the one in his soul, he saw a lit window a long way across from him. With a curiosity in the lives of others, he went to get the telescope that had been part of a bundle of possessions one of his friends had left with him for safekeeping.

He found a view of a staircase, leading up to what he assumed were the bedroom and bathroom. He sat in the dark, with no ambitions or interests, becoming the view, nothing but that tondo, wondering if he could learn anything about life from observing others in secret; was there a trick he was missing?

A form shot up the stairs and into the room on the left. An impression that, after its disappearance, he decided must be womanly; he redoubled his seeing, sitting patiently for what was thirty minutes but seemed less. She went into the bathroom. He saw the light fill the opaque window. The probability that to some extent she must be undressing started to strangle him.

He sat unmoving for what felt like a long time because it was an hour and a half—but then he was rewarded with a flicker of her body moving from room to room, which he was able to reconstitute as her wearing only her underwear. Of course, any number of alternatives were available to him to obtain far franker vistas of far nakeder, far more attractive women. But this glimpse made him tremble uncontrollably.

"Misuse, welcome," he remarked to himself.

He would take up his position late at night when he had a chance of catching her at her ablutions. Daylight brought down the shutters, but darkness offered light. He logged her undergarments, color, cut. Time in the bathroom. Time the bedroom light went out. His eye buried itself in the ridges of the wallpaper between the two rooms, it studied the cracks on the bannisters, the fiber of the carpet as it waited for the target. He became that staircase, waited with the patience of carpet for her footsteps.

Then there was the great day when she paused at the top, topless, then went downstairs; the pause was only a few seconds, but it was to take more room in his memory than entire years. Excitement wrestled him to the floor. At the age of forty-two he had accidentally recaptured the strength and novelty of a thirteen-year-old's passion.

He was a little ashamed of what he did, but he was intruding no more than the light; the telescope merely rendered up more detail, while the substance of the pictures was there for anyone with good eyesight. And it took a considerable investment of time. He fretted when she came home late, grieved when she went on holiday, marveled at the time she spent in the bathroom.

"No one gets hurt," he said, realizing that much of the

pleasure was this, his pleasure couldn't jostle her life, there could be no collisions.

Day and light meant little to him; only with the advent of darkness did his blood start pumping. He wished he could get her out of the bathroom, stripped for vision. Then one day in his mail he found a misdelivered letter, with a name, and an address he realized could well be her house. He walked around the block and counted. Sure enough it was hers. As he skulked, she came out of the house; it was a perfect opportunity to meet, how considerate he would look delivering the letter. But he decided that the telescope was better. He waited till she had gone before he dropped the letter in.

But he sprinted to the telephone directory and checked her name. It was there. It occurred to him if her phone was downstairs, he could ring when she was in the bathroom and if she thought the call important—as you might well do with a late night call—she would rush down without much in the way of clothing.

The thought incapacitated him. He tried the number to make sure it worked. He had to lie down all day in expectation, only able to take fluids. He took up his position hours early. He waited with elbows sore from leaning on his desk for her to go into the bathroom. He counted off a few minutes, let the water run, look in the mirror, fiddle with hair, inspect cosmetics, fiddle with armpits, squeeze some comedones, slip off some vestments, then he dialed the number, heard the ringing.

She came downstairs, with no blouse on, but wearing a new bra. He was delirious. The knowledge that he had the power to flush her out unbalanced him. Just this ephemeral flash of flesh was as great an erotic treasure as his most clingy and aquaterreous liaisons.

He used it rarely though. Firstly he was afraid she might

146

change her number if it were abused, and secondly the evenings when she didn't show or when nothing worthwhile was shown made the moments when a bare leg would dangle out of the bathroom and consider its course all the more efficacious. You had to pay with tedium for the peaks.

He observed and relished all the minutiae of her life. He disapproved of late-night gentlemen callers, but they didn't last. He anonymously sent her silk scarves and other presents and enjoyed watching her put them on, as well as taking them off. He found himself whistling a lot, and his friends remarked how full of good humor he was.

Then one evening, as he called, he saw her dash out, wearing the earrings he had sent, which represented going on your own to a party where you know no one; he saw her fall down the stairs. Her neck was broken.

Lettuce Again

"I can't believe it," says Lettuce, "I'm sitting on the train reading some diaries from the First World War, when these two idiots start fighting. They grasp each other by the lapels, roll over on top of me, and start headbutting each other. They're big, and I'm underneath them as they reach unconsciousness together. My diary's covered in blood. I missed my stop because I couldn't get out from under them. I mean, what's going on here?" She takes out a lid-twisting device from her bag and has a go at the jar of beetroot.

"Don't ask me," says Rosa.

"I'm looking forward to the day when men will be replaced by sachets of sperm. No more wars. No more crime. Why's there a FOR SALE sign outside? Are you moving?"

"No, it must be someone upstairs. Or just those shits sticking up signs everywhere trying to convince everyone there's a recovery. So what have you come to complain about?"

"What makes you think I've come to complain?" gasps Lettuce, dropping the beetroot and wheeling on the full tub of coleslaw.

"Well, the fact that every time you come to see me you complain ceaselessly from the moment you cross the threshold, unless it's to eat something or to ask to borrow something."

"No, that's not true," she says, affronted. "Let's talk about you, Rosa. How are you?"

"I'm fine, apart from the odd hired killer making a mess on my floor."

"Do you know what he said to me last night?"

"No."

"He said, The thing I enjoy most about you sucking my cock is that you can't talk."

"I can't imagine why."

"Don't you think that's a terrible thing to say?"

"Yes, it is. Tell me, Lettuce, is this the guy you met at Kew?"

"Yeah."

"Is my recollection right that this is the man whose opening gambit was: 'Stay away from me, I'm a complete bastard'?"

"Yes."

"So you met someone, who by your own account is not good-looking, a self-confessed Mr. Wrong, who goes on to relate that two of his girlfriends have committed suicide. And now—if I'm mistaken, please correct me—you're sitting here complaining to me because he hasn't been very nice to you."

"But why do men have to behave like that? And they

never stay anymore. He just drops by—whummp—he shoots off and then . . . shoots off. We don't go out anywhere."

"Lettuce, let me give you this tenner."

"Why?"

"Because you can have it as long as you don't mention that you might be pregnant, that you prefer to get it right to the back of your mouth so you can't taste it going down, and that men don't seem to get any better."

"Don't be nasty. If you can't get sympathy from your friends, who can you?"

"You can have my sympathy anytime." She gives Lettuce a hug. "You can have it anytime, just ask for it, and you can have it; but don't feel you have to solicit it, because it won't work." Lettuce overshadows the potato salad.

"What bothers me is that he's going out with someone else from the faculty."

"Another historian?"

"Yes, and she looks like me, she's got short dark hair. What's she got that I haven't? I asked him. 'She's just like you, really,' he said, 'that's what I like about her; but she's younger and she's got tits.' I think he was trying to be kind."

"I admire you," Lettuce says, "I really do. You just don't get worked up about any of this. You're so good at being single."

"Do you want me to fix you something?"

"No," says Lettuce, peering in at the hummus, "but do you have any bread?"

"Yes, over there. I wish things could be different. You're almost murdered, you carry out a failed kidnapping, and then you have to do the dusting. It's so boring, doing your own dusting. You should be able to come up with some system where you get to do your neighbor's dusting, so you

149

can see some different photographs, hangings, calico, see a different view out the window, have different tricky ledges to clean."

Rosa is right. World history is largely comprehensible through the study of who did the dusting. Agriculture, medicine, warfare has changed out of all recognition, but there is no substitute for the old biddy going in with the old shirt. Tourism is the other catalyst, of course; you want to see the world, so you join a marauding horde.

"Failed kidnapping?" Lettuce asks, teasing out the last of the hummus.

"Just joking."

"The sex is good, but it's not great."

"Did I ask that?"

"Don't be nasty. Can't I talk?"

"What do you expect? He couldn't be a complete bastard, really, however hard he pretends, otherwise he wouldn't have warned you. He's only a half-finished complete bastard."

"Who's a complete bastard?" says Nikki, arriving.

"Lettuce's new beau's almost there."

"Complete bastards, love 'em." Nikki takes in Lettuce, not having met her. "Four minutes," she says. "That is if we're talking about rumpy-pumpy delivery. Not worried about flowers or stimulating conversation. I used to meet one at ten-thirty prompt Friday night at someone else's flat on the other side of London, Hornchurch. For half an hour. Just for the florida. Think he'd told his wife he'd just gone out for a quick one. He was only good for one thing, but he was good at that one thing. They're the best thing when it comes to the world of muff. Complete bastards and second nights."

"Second nights?" inquires Lettuce.

"Yeah second nights. Assuming the first one worked properly. But it's the second night, when everything fits together but you've still got that novelty. Freshness and teamwork. Then it's mostly downhill."

"Maybe. Is this wine any good?" Lettuce says, peeking into the fridge. The wine is dispensed liberally.

"Why is it so hard to find a man?" inquires Lettuce. "Even getting competent sex can take more work than it's worth."

"Maybe it's always been like this," proposes Rosa. "Perhaps the truth is that even in the Rift Valley women sat around complaining, not getting men, not getting the men they like, not being able to get rid of the men they didn't like. Maybe you're born with dreams, but the dreams are there to be trampled, they're your insulation, the wrapping to keep out life's grubby mitts, to help get you toward the end of your life. I remember my mother doing the dishes one evening and saying to me, 'Don't fall for this.' If you knew what was coming, no one would leave the womb. Cesareans all around."

"More likely to be murdered by someone who loved you once," remarks Lettuce, as if discussing her future.

"Yeah, I don't know what's going on these days," interposes Nikki. "I ended up screwing this Brazilian transsexual before the operation. I didn't understand a word he, or she, said. He had tits and a cock—well not much, it was daintied out by the treatment. You know he really wanted to be fuhked by some bodybuilder, but I was there with this uncomfortable strap-on because there was nothing much on television, pumping away in his rear end. It's not doing much for me, frankly, he was screaming something I couldn't understand, something I thought was Brazilian, then I remembered it was the name I was using at the time. Things are just so complicated nowadays."

"I know the feeling," says Rosa. "Do you know that Lump is still sitting out there? How did your job interviews go?"

The drink drives them deep into the night. They invite in Lump, who sits silently as a bowl. Nikki tackles Lettuce on the origin of her name. Lettuce apparently spent her scholarship money buying a car for her boyfriend, forcing her to scavenge from the market for stray fruit and orphaned vegetables for a year.

"What happened to the boyfriend?"

"He drove off."

It is three fourteen when Rosa comes to me for her bedtime story. I de-file once about the defilement of love. . . .

The Trumpeter

He would be seen in the company, always, of his favorite pig, which he called Pig. He had a dog, called Dog, and his wife had a cat, Cat.

One day he woke up and realized he had to be rid of his wife. He decided an accident would look good. He often sent her to visit her sister, who lived on the other side of the river—particularly in bad weather. The ferry, which often sank, never sank when she was on. He sent her to visit her brother, who lived on the other side of the county, but somehow the brigands always missed her.

He gave her poisons, inserted into the food; he fell ill and she would attend to him sympathetically. He took her clothes to people dying from horrible diseases and made them wear them. He fell ill and she would attend to him sympathetically.

They went for walks by the cliffs. "Come and have a look at this, it's fascinating," he would say.

"You're too close to the edge," his prudent wife would say.

"No, this is amazing. You must have a look at this," he said on one occasion as he craned and slipped over the edge. He was fortunate in that he fell only twenty feet onto a ledge and only had to suffer the agony of a broken leg for two hours before they managed to lower a rope to him. His wife attended to him sympathetically.

He went to the chief of a local band of brigands with most of his savings in gold coin. "My wife will be traveling on this path at this time. I hope you will accept this offering and take my suggestion that you might ambush her party, ravish her by all means, but do take her life. She does have some superb chryselephantine jewelry."

"Very interesting," said the chief, "but I have a question for you. What is there to stop me taking your money, laughing contemptuously at you, tying you to that tree over there, flogging you until you have been half-flayed, and then taking bets on whether or not you'll live?"

"Nothing."

"That's what I thought."

Miraculously, he managed to crawl back home, losing most of the skin that remained on the front of his elbows and knees, and he spent the next months lying in bed, in agony no matter which side he tried. His wife attended to him sympathetically.

He gave her strong drink, put her to bed, and then started a fire. Returning, as if from a long walk, he started shouting once the flames had taken good hold. The entire house burned down, leaving only the bed, his wife without a singed hair, her trunk full of her favorite clothes, and a remarkably resilient and good-looking pitcher. His favorite pig was over-done. They went to live with his wife's sister, who had never liked him much.

One day, he went to see the local physician and gave him a large present, with money he had borrowed.

"What can I do for you?" the physician inquired. "Water-works, is it?"

"Nothing. Nothing at all. I simply feel you're not appreciated enough, and I just enjoy your company. Now tell me, have you heard the story about the fellow, I can't remember his name, who lived in that town, I can't recall exactly where, but I heard he found this ingenious way of killing his wife? It was very, very clever because no one suspected a thing, there were no traces of violence or poison; it was very, very clever, but for the life of me I can't remember now how he did it. Does this ring a bell with you?"

"Ah, an ingenious, dastardly method of killing his wife. Yes, I think I know the story you mean. A very popular story. I can't remember his name or where he lived either, but the method he chose was indeed most ingenious; he applied himself to his wife's nethermouth and blew mightily into it, like a trumpet, a long fanfare, the pressured air engendering what we call embolism, which arrests the heart as if in a great passion."

"Any particular tune?"

"Whatever you fancy. But don't forget: As in any musicianship, practice is the key. Diligence. What can it not achieve? Oh, my birthday's next month, by the way. I'm very fond of goose."

He went to his wife's bedchamber and huffed and puffed. His ardor bewildered his wife. An ardor which didn't diminish over the following weeks; she had to encourage him to take meals. At the end of the month he puffed out his life into her privates.

"It's always one or the other," remarked the physician. "Pity about the goose."

Ooooooff come the hands.

But Rosa still looks at me. Sleep is not making any headway; insatiability is sovereign. Women can make an ooooooooooo without end; it is always men who pull the plug

154

on their pleasure. I have much more stock, but every time she takes a plunge, she gets closer to the truth, and I begin to suspect that her fondness for the past is becoming an addiction. The past, the future—they're the tourist attractions. The present is the poor relation of time; it has to carry the can for all sorts of tribulations.

Oooooon come the hands.

The Hole

She was betrothed to the biggest boy in the village. He spent his time punching smaller boys or, when he got tired of that, dictating elaborate schemes for the boys to pulverize one another. "Right hook, left uppercut; now squeeze his balls, ordure, or I'll come and do it for you."

His other preferred pastime was describing in graphic detail what he would do to his bride, so no one in the village would have any queries about the wedding night. He would be seen wandering around the village, thrusting his hips vigorously into the air and waggling his tongue in contortions of ecstasy. No one was allowed to look at his bride. "I don't even want anyone thinking about thinking about it," he said, pausing to think about what he had said to verify that it was right. "Or thinking about thinking about thinking about it." Ruthlessly stupid, the Air Humper could have a claim to inventing the bidet when he said, "Lick my arse"; it was unfigurative.

His betrothed was beautiful. She was also so good-natured that she couldn't believe her prospective groom was so bad, and she was too good-natured to complain about the match.

"You are so beautiful," the boy with the charmingest cock in the village said to her. When he had been born, the midwife had pronounced, "He'll never get married, not with that." All the mothers had encouraged their daughters to play with him, though they were too young to know why.

"All women are beautiful, but some only for a few minutes," Charmingest continued. "And it might be at night or when no one is around. You are so lucky—you will be beautiful for every moment of your life."

The good-natured girl smiled because it was a skillful compliment and because he needed balls the size of kegs to make it; her smile was not one of encouragement, but it was so good-natured, it acted as such.

"I can't look at other girls. I'd like to, because many of them are pretty and it would be much safer. You see that pair of old nags harnessed together"—here Charmingest pointed at a pair of consumptive horses—"see how their bones stick out. They are famished and worn, blinkered, but they lean on each other. They have everything because they have each other. I would like us to be like that."

Charmingest might have made reference to a simple, but glorious in its simplicity, jug that was nearby. He might have drawn an image from the flawless perfection of its body, but he didn't. Such is often the unappreciated fate of perfection.

The good-natured girl smiled again. It was another great compliment, the likes of which had not been heard in the region for a hundred years. A secret admirer was fun. She wanted to show him her breasts as a reward, but that wouldn't have been a wise idea.

"I thought about bringing you flowers, but that would be too easy," said Charmingest (and too dangerously visible). "I've decided to dig you the largest hole in the world." She smiled and wondered what he meant, but it was exactly that.

The war came, against the people who spoke the same language and who looked like the people in the village; it came so suddenly there was no time for a ceremony. Air Humper, the lugal-in-making, strapped on his war-making paraphernalia while making powerful thrusts of his loins and making it clear which parts of the good-natured girl would be getting his closest attention on his return.

Meanwhile, every day for an hour or so, Charmingest would dig in a barren, uncultivated, poorly irrigated patch of land outside the village. At first no one noticed, but by the time he was down to this shoulders, people turned up. "What are you doing?" they asked.

"I'm digging for treasure," he'd reply. Some believed him and joined in the digging for a few days, but mostly it was an opportunity to get their jerkins off in front of the village girls.

"Are you sure there's something here?"

"I'm sure," Charmingest would say. He was soon left on his own.

The wars went on. The two armies missed each other. Chased each other around mountains, took the wrong valleys, confused rivers, overtook each other, walked past each other in the night, bumped into other armies they hadn't been expecting, wiped them out, were snowed in, and then kept on missing each other, and there was talk that the two generals who led the armies weren't in any rush to get back because their wives were nags, but they didn't mind; there were genial massacres, old gold such as torturing prisoners to death when things were slow, and marvelous discoveries, such as juggling stoats.

Finally, the reckoning. Everyone agreed it was one of the best battles that had ever been fought, much much better than the battles their fathers had fought and talked about, and much better than any that would come. Air Humper even drew a spontaneous standing ovation from the opposing army for the inventiveness of his brutality.

Air Humper returned at night, eager to get thrusting,

walking over land he had known since he could walk, laden down with booty (including a golden penis sheath bearing the legend WHAT ARE YOU LOOKING AT?) and grumbling about his toothache when he fell into a twenty-foot hole he hadn't been expecting and broke his neck.

People were upset but not that much, since there wasn't going to be another war for an interwar. The hole was the biggest thing anyone had ever seen. Charmingest married the good-natured girl; the success of their union was demonstrated by her screams ringing out across the village at night, much valued by couples and those on their own alike.

However, it all came to an untimely end one night when a rain of icy iguanas decimated the village.

A small lake formed in the hole. It was said in the environs for a long time afterward that sweethearts who swam together in the altogether in the lake would stay together for life.

Ooooooff hands.

Rosa falls asleep, thinking of the lake.

What Is This?

Well-dreamed, Rosa springs out of bed the next morning, and we go to see some suits who are gathered in a worried way round some coins. Rosa picks up the gold pieces and rubs them. There are fifty-eight coins. She accords each coin a due time, but I can see what's coming. She ponders for a moment, not because she needs to ponder, but because she's building up.

"They're about as Lydian as my arse," she evaluates. She's enjoying this.

The oldest suit, who was struggling to restrain his unhappiness, lets it fly. He has the biggest nose I've seen for a hundred and seventy-two years, though with noses you always have to, strictly, divide them into weight and volume. Everyone else in the room is wondering how he manages to stand up with a hooter like that.

"This is absurd. Absurd. How anyone can take seriously an assessment like that?"

Grandfather Suit is vexed, but whatever the others may think of Rosa and her judgement, the spirit of purchase has flown out of the window. Doubt breeds quietly. Rosa reaches into her purse and hands frothing Grandfather her card, which I know has the following inscription:

> No publicity.
> No fuss.
> No cheques.
> And absolutely no debate.

"I'll give you this as a bonus; they were made within the last twenty years, probably within the last ten." She has the confidence of someone who knows they can do one thing better than anyone else alive.

A younger suit, red-faced, counts out ten twenty-pound notes into Rosa's hand.

We return as Nikki is showing out a couple. Earnest money-earners, sports-club members. They smile in a show of politeness as they pass, Nikki quite deliberately suppressing the introductions.

"Who were they?" Rosa asks.

"Oh, Jehovah's Witnesses."

"You're very fond of them."

159

"I feel sorry for them, traipsing around and everyone shutting the door in their faces. Helen called; she said she needs the bowl."

Marius's chauffeur turns up with another vase. A Gorgon vase.

Accident ahoy. That's the thing—you can go hundreds of years without seeing one, then they all trail in together.

"He's already bought this one, but he wants you to give it the once over."

The chauffeur then presents a bunch of flowers to Nikki. "I wanted to say thank you. When you called him a withered turd, it was the best moment of my life. If you do meet him again, I do hope you won't hold back."

Rosa stares into space. She is thinking about giving up. There comes a point where you want to give up, either because you're not keen on getting what you want anymore or because you know you're not going to get it or that it's going to cost more than it should, but you keep going, not through strength but through default, because there's nothing else you can do.

Nikki is trying to reach a lightbulb in the hallway to change it, not out of any altruism but because she likes looking at herself in the mirror there. She stands on a chair but she is short, the ceiling is high.

"You can't reach this?" asks Nikki.

"No. I always have to be nice to someone tall: I've returned the ladder I borrowed."

"How many angels does it take to change a lightbulb?" Nikki muses, going outside to fetch Lump, who takes care of the task. "While you're here, you might as well open this jar of beetroot."

"It won't work," says Rosa.

"Course it will," says Nikki, offering the jar to Lump.

Lump applies metal-bending force, but the lid remains inscrutable. The jar shatters, releasing beetroot to do its worst.

"I told you. You can try too hard. I glued it so it would slow Lettuce down. You're welcome to have a cup of tea, Lump, or to sit here."

"I'm fine outside." She turns to Nikki. "Aren't things better this way?"

"Yeah. Great," says Nikki, closing the door on her.

"Why didn't you get her to stay?" asks Rosa, after Lump has left.

"She's having her fun. Sitting in a van's quite cheap as hobbies go."

"How exactly did you meet?"

"In a supermarket. My lemons got mixed up with her shopping. We were at the checkout."

Restoration: What Nikki is trying not to say is that she doubtless attempted to steal Lump's lemons, having forgotten to shop for them herself. No object too small, probably no object too large, to purloin.

"We got chatting."

Restoration: bone-breaking sexual practices.

"Then I stayed at her place for a while."

Suddenly I see that the balance has changed; Nikki unsettled Rosa. Now Rosa unsettles Nikki; only rocks are hard all the way through. Nothing to do with this conversation, but it is plain.

"There were benefits." Indeed, one can imagine the assets being stripped.

Lump and Nikki

"When I was at Lump's, I came back one night and this scumbag must have been hanging around the subway waiting

161

for shaggable single women. I get home exhausted, get into bed, turn off the light, drop off. Then I started to surface as you do in the morning, but it was still dark, and there was another warmth next to me in the bed, breathing on my back, and a strong smell of aftershave. I felt stubble on the back of my neck, I searched my memory for a pickup, 'cause it occurred to me that Lump would go berserk if she found us together; then I saw from the clock on the table I'd only been asleep for ten minutes and whoever was there wasn't there at my invitation. I wondered what the hell to do, because it was a large warmth. I could tell he was awake and enjoying it. I also knew he'd be able to tell I wasn't asleep by my breathing and tensing. We waited for what must have been a few minutes, till his breathing became gasping. Then a kitchen knife came round my throat.

"He believed in foreplay, he held it there and got off on it. I actually wondered if he was going to bother, but then he spread my legs and we were about to get on with it when Lump got in from work and disturbed us.

"He was cool. He was turned on by this. You could see him thinking, Never shagged anything half the size of that. 'Strip,' he said, waving the knife. So Lump broke his arm, an old habit from her work as a bouncer. 'You hit people in the head, you're always risking paperwork and long court appearances; break their arm, everyone just thinks it's funny,' as she always used to say. But then she thought about it and threw him against the wall, so hard a dent appeared. I'd reckon the only reason she didn't do it again was because she didn't want to damage the wall anymore.

"Our friend was not in a fit state to whack a fly, he was blubbering on the floor, saying he was going to call the police. I was wondering whether to kick him in the head or the balls when Lump got the bondage gear, stuck a gag on him, tied him down, and then got out the really huge strap-on, the massive purple one with lifelike veins, the one you wouldn't think anyone would ever use, just give as the novelty present at hen-nights. Lump put it on and went to town on him. I thought his eyeballs were going to pop out and roll around the floor. She gave it to him until the early hours of morning; she said she lost a stone from the exertion. The way he looked in the morning when the police turned up, I felt sorry for him."

The rapist raped; such neatness, such justice is rare. Rare as the frozen iguanas. It is a story that has strayed into life. This is why it's told.

I am tucked up in Rosa's bed. Now she is going to want life as a story. I am ready with a pastoral epic with a cast of thousands and breathtaking landscapes. Oooooon come the hands.

The Village That Wasn't

No one came to the village.

The other villages all had talking points. Some had good harvests, others intricate embroidery. The village down the river was famous for the funny-shaped vegetables that always grew there. Carrots in the shape of donkeys, a parsnip that looked just like the lugal of the locale, which had been presented to him and had earned the bearers extreme largesse (though some pointed out, very quietly, it was more that the lugal looked like a parsnip, rather than the parsnip resembling the lugal), onions indistinguishable from a fevered couple in congress.

The village up the river had a wolf that rode on horseback, a magpie that drank beer, and it was rumored they had stoats who they'd trained to juggle.

The village at the foot of the mountain made dreadful wine, but they had a man called Funnel. He was called Funnel because he could drink any quantity of wine, kilderkin after kilderkin, at one go. People in his village had tried to keep up with him; they had fallen violently ill, and the more assiduous had died. Topers from nearby villages came to drink against him. They died, usually after only two kilderkins. The more prudent paid for his kilderkins, watching him play the aqueduct, in the hope that he would expire. Naturally, after three or four kilderkins he would part company with his consciousness, but his assistants would lay him on his back, insert a funnel into his mouth and pour in wine till the onlookers' money was spent.

(Much of my professional time has been spent in the company of determined drinkers, either as krater or skyphos, and I must say here that the Funnel was by far the greatest dipsomaniac I have encountered—and don't forget, I was around when grapes and grain were viewed as just handy things for folks to eat. It was a great pity, considering his talents, that he had such a small and rustic public. I often wondered whether he was really human, but I have yet to find firmer evidence of an alien culture that likes to have fifteen-year benders on other planets.)

The Funnel almost single-handedly consumed the village's wine output, which was just as well since, as you had to be near suicidal to even contemplate it, the consumption would have otherwise been modest. In the end, one year when the harvest failed, he perished on his way to another village, desperate for a drink. But while the Funnel was in action, the flow of visitors brought revenue, and every now and then when they had established a visitor wasn't endowed with rich, powerful, violent, or vindictive kin, they would have some fun and torture and murder, and use any remains as fertilizer.

The people in the village without side-splitting vegetables, juggling stoats, or the finest drunk in world history would gather in the evenings, before they would pass out from their toil, and would moan about how they were never talked about, never had any visitors, let alone the chance of abusing them.

"We've got to do something to become more interesting."

"No, first we have to become interesting, before we can even think about becoming more interesting."

They had nearly the same conversation every evening, but different people said the same lines. Then, one evening a poor, ugly girl from a neighboring village, who had only got married to the chief thresher because she had thought the squalor might be more vivid in another village suggested: "Why don't we do something, then?"

There was a silence. No one in the village had ever had an idea before. But the girl didn't know this, and so she continued: "Why don't we start living at night and sleep during the day? We will become known as those who live in darkness. People might think we have riveting dark powers." There was a long silence, mostly because she had interrupted the same conversation they had always had and now no one could remember what came next. It took several weeks for them to think of thinking about it, but then they went wild with the joy of invention and took up the suggestion.

The topsy-turviness lasted for ten days. It stopped because people kept injuring themselves, the farmers couldn't get their furrows right and because the neighboring folk, much perplexed by what was going on, start coming round during the day to steal chickens and anything not nailed down. They switched back but felt proud that they had been talked about.

"So what are we going to do to be even more interesting?"

everyone would say now in the evenings, slapping each other on the back since, although they weren't known as those who live in the darkness, they were known even more intriguingly as those who sometimes live in the darkness, but when you least expect it and not for very long. They were overwhelmed by their success.

"Why don't we change the name of the village?" suggested the girl after six months of these extremely repetitive congratulations. She had decided that her life was going to be short and ghastly so that it might as well be short and ghastly in a larger place where accidentally she might have a laugh before she died. She decided to leave the next day.

The village's name at that time was simply "the village that isn't the village at the foot of the mountain nor the village that's further down the river but not the village that's further up the river either"; or even more simply, "the village that isn't."

"Why don't we change the name of the village to Arsehole?" she said.

"Why would we do that?" they asked incredulously.

"Because it's funny. If there were a village called Arsehole, wouldn't you go along to jeer? People will come here, and you can sell them mead."

She waited as they thought it over, wondering if anyone would be clever enough to point out that changing the name to something evocative such as the Ultimate Truth, or Fascination's Finest Flowering or The Really Good Place They Don't Want You to Know About might have the same effect but without the ignominy.

She left the day after they changed the name. Visitors did come and snigger, although one look was enough for them and they purchased niggardly amounts of mead.

Eventually, as always, the marauders arrived. They had

already impaled two interpreters, who, on being asked if there was anywhere else left to pillage, had replied: "Arsehole." The marauders were outraged by its dullness. They burned down the village and made everyone jump up and down on the ashes for a day. They located the village shit and offered him his life if he'd kill everyone else in the village.

"How would you like the job done?"

They gave him a spoon.

"What am I supposed to do with that?"

"Use your imagination."

"It'll take a while."

"We're in no rush."

The spoon is small, and the shrieks are large, yet the truth is the marauders don't pay too much attention, because they can't get enough of the juggling stoats.

Tabatha's Do

Essentially, I have grown a pair of legs.

Rosa takes me everywhere. We go to Tabatha's soiree, where I am dumped in a bedroom and interred under several overcoats, bags, and their owners' spoors. The mingling is at the other end of the flat so even my acute hearing can't pick up the vocal detail through the smog of chatter, but I don't worry, because if Rosa is going to put her hands in my mnemonic pockets later on, I'm going to do the same. Drearily, nothing lewd or improper takes place in the bedroom, and I am retrieved after a few hours.

At home, I see Rosa is so pleased and inebriated I prognosticate that she will go straight for the Zs; but in bed, she turns to me and stretches out her hands.

I give her the Koreans Who Tried to Eat China or the Three Stomachs Against an Empire.

167

I backflip into her head, and the memory is there like a doormat:

"No, I always start at the balls," says the girl, enjoying the undivided attention of the men gathered around her, forcing themselves to look as if they are quite used to such candorous discussion. The girl is a well-known type. Many men hover around; they are scrubbed, professional, with money and leisure time for health clubs, wine collections. Their clothes strain to give hints of loucheness and unprofessionalism, but these are people who work to three decimal places, and that always shows.

By the avocado dip, Rosa is cornered by a solicitor with gold-rim glasses, with a face rounded not by overeating but by fate. His chin juts out, giving an air of determination and smugness. I shoot through the Ping-Pong conversation, the exchange of counters to the end of the evening, as they build a picture of their lives.

The Chin (Forty Thousand One Hundred and Nine) makes jokes about the art world; Rosa makes the standard jokes about solicitors (and remember, you can never go wrong shooting a lawyer). You can see Rosa is anxious that he might do something unforgivably disgusting or not go for the proposal. Tabatha beams from the other side of the room, as Rosa's number is written down.

Back home, Rosa doesn't leave the flat, which is odd since there is nothing to eat; she paces up and down restlessly. I educe she is waiting for a phone call, since every forty minutes or so she picks up the receiver to reassure herself the line is operational. Finally, after mooching for eleven hours and twenty-six minutes, fearful that she is part of the phoning rather than the phoned, the phone rings. She counts up to ten before answering it and then suggesting supper in the fourth most fashionable restaurant in London.

Nevertheless, the next day Rosa thinks better of going out for supper; she rings him up and invites him to a Rosa-cooked supper. Which, as we all know, means only one thing.

"Nikki," says Rosa. "Could you make sure you're out *all* Wednesday night?"

"Home entertainment? Is he big?"

"A bit chunky."

"That's good. Let's not pretend. A big man's small willy is better than a small man's big willy."

She cooks the day before. The house is cleaned feverishly; she stays up till two in the morning grouting the bathroom and tracking down oddly-placed, recalcitrant stains in the kitchen. "I should do this anyway," she says. She dusts the lightbulbs and repaints a corner of the front-room's door.

Tabatha phones: "Don't rush. I think the message is clear; nothing speaks more frankly than lamb stew."

The Chin arrives. Rosa lets him in with that smile women reserve for men who are going to be driving them home, but the smile teeters and falls off a cliff when she sees a woman with him.

"Hello, Rosa. This is my wife, Jacky. Hope you don't mind, but she wanted to come along."

"Not at all," says Rosa, the courtesy coming out by itself. "Come on in."

The Chins do the talking, aware that Rosa is winded. She serves the starter, a wild mushroom tartlet, which is eulogized by her guests. She draws to a halt.

"Look, I apologize, but I can't go on with this. I assumed Simon was single. Sorry, but there's no point."

"The stew does smell delicious though," says the female Chin.

"I'm not hungry."

"Honestly, Rosa, my being married doesn't make me

169

any different. Let's eat and then we can talk about the arrangements."

"The arrangements?"

"Let's not be shy. You find me attractive. I find you attractive. We all need *l'amour*. We can let nature take its course, and Jacky can watch."

"Obviously," says Jacky, *"l'amour* is something we all need. Let me just say, Rosa, I find you very attractive, and I'll be very happy in any creative position."

"I'd like you to leave."

"Would you like to watch us—inspect the merchandise, as it were?"

"No."

"I must say, Rosa, your attitude is most offensive. Jacky's too polite to say anything, but just imagine how she must feel by your out-of-hand rejection."

Rosa demonstrates how the door works.

"You're right. We're being a little push-push-pushy, aren't we? But I think you'll find there is nothing on television tonight. Idea: We'll go to the pub on the corner. Here's my cell phone number—if you change your mind, give us a ring. And you must give me the recipe for the tartlet."

Rosa sits on the sofa and hugs herself as hard as she can.

For so long, the bulk of celebration has fallen on those called successful: the rich, the speedy, the lugals, the top-of-the-pile people. It's sooooooo misleading, because they're not as free from torment as many imagine and because they're so unrepresentative.

The rulers, the flourishing, the superlativists: They're the freaks. It is the also-rans, the unmedaled ice-skaters, the bankrupt philatelists, the embittered inventors, the self-hating civil servants, those with talent and education and determination who potter along; these are the ones who should be made into examples, so that people can see their lives aren't benighted but standard. Beating back your life with drink or drugs shouldn't be a national sport.

For every champion, there are a thousand competitors and another two thousand would-be competitors who forget to turn up, or had a cold, or were sulking over a love affair or couldn't be bothered to get an application form. It is the champions who know nothing of life. Winning is not life, fighting for third place is. But, of course, the commissions come from those with brass, the victors, and the losers like to study the victors because they think they might pick up something. What's the difference between the man with millions and the man without millions? Millions.

What should be imbibed is not how to achieve success, which, by definition, is the preserve of a few, but how to see the colors of failure's eyes without flinching, how to tolerate the foul breath of ordinariness. The person on the pedestal should be the unmoaning decorator who has lost his business, who even when he shoplifts a small bottle of whiskey is caught, who after thirty years of work has nothing but mottled overalls to show for it while his daughter, his only joy, is unskillfully tapped by a penniless brute; it is the cleaning woman with children to support who, going home late, exhausted, has her earnings stolen on the subway who can provide important lessons: how to lose.

Rosa chooses a postcard and first addresses it to her sister; then chews the pen while she searches for the phrase. All I know about her sister is what she mentioned to Nikki during cup of tea fourteen: "She married the first boy she went out with. Can you imagine that?" Rosa gnaws sixteen-minutedly and then writes: "You were right."

Then Rosa takes an early mattress. She lies quietly for an hour or so, unable to roll her mind into the black. Her hands reach ooooooooout. I feel she wants something to prolong the poignancy.

Nose

"They're all the same," they said at the seamstress's. The older women were the worst. She felt ashamed and stupid in defending her husband.

"What makes you think he's any different?" they cackled. "Is he a hunchback without a tool? That's the only thing that would keep him from climbing onto other women, and even then he'd be trying."

The older women dripped bitterness. Their husbands had cheated on them with varying levels of discretion, interspersed with heavy drinking and blows; the most worthless had betrayed them by dying. Of the fifteen women who worked there, only the Mole had a quiet, sober, hard-working husband (and he was dying of consumption). And her.

"The best you can hope for is that he doesn't do it under your nose," they croned.

Her husband had courted her with both courtesy and passion. They had gone on walks so long they got lost, walks so long they returned in the dark. He had simmered respectfully, but when he had taken her hand, her whole skin had tightened in exultation.

She had attracted much ridicule on account of her nose, long and aquiline. On their wedding night, her husband ran through the inventory. "Your toes I want to protect. Your navel I want to lick. Your hair is wonderful. Your breasts are the perfect size. No one could ask for more. But your nose. Your nose is why I love you and why I married you."

She slapped him, persuaded that he was making fun of her nose as everyone else had done. She cried until the tears

172

dried. But he soon showed her that his rhinophilia was not a jest, as he did things she had never dreamt of but she soon grew to be fond of.

With him, she always felt close and safe. Without the constant slurs on his fidelity she endured at work, it would never have occurred to her to doubt him.

Once, she borrowed a friend's headscarf and followed him one evening at a distance, and saw him go to a tavern and spend hours with friends. A young woman joined them, and she could see that, while the other men joked with the newcomer, there was no room in his body for more uninterest. Her husband yawned and left the group.

He would spend hours with the children, helping them with reading. When she didn't have the time, he would carry cakes over to her mother. She was the one who urged him to buy new clothes. His clothes were good, but old and threadbare. "Why spend the money?" he said. "These clothes have been loyal. Besides, I don't have to impress the ladies anymore." The household was modest, the only item of real value being a superb porcelain vase given to them by a friend with unusually good taste.

Then she realized that he could only be so indifferent to the young girl, so helpful to her, so indifferent to his appearance, because he already had a mistress. She followed him around, and because she found nothing, she became all the more convinced of his infidelity, since the absence of evidence meant he must be hiding it. How could he account for every coin he spent unless he knew he would be facing scrutiny?

One evening, he came home late by half an hour, saying he had tried to see a dentist because of toothache. She accused him of lying. He got angry and threw the vase. It was the only time he had been late, the only time he had been angry with her. But you only have to be angry once to become an angry man, just as a vase that breaks once is always broken. A vase has its cracks to remind it; he had his wife.

Hands ooooooff.

The phone is ringing. This is annoying because I was about to get didactic.

Rosa answers. It is a reverse-charge call.

"From Nigeria?" She is puzzled; it is two in the morning and she knows no one in Nigeria, but fearing something of importance, she accepts the call.

"Hello," says the voice, "I have a business proposition for you."

"I think you have the wrong number," says Rosa.

"No, no, we met six months ago."

"What's my name then?" inquired Rosa.

"I remember you very well."

"You have the wrong number."

"No, let me tell you quickly about this business proposition."

"Please listen carefully: I don't know who you are, but I do know you're an arsehole."

She slams the phone down and goes to the television and watches it, although there's nothing on. It is a knife feebly peeling the darkness of the world. She is carrying so much whiskey that two hours later when she destinates toward bed, she barely makes it. I hate interrupted narration. Perhaps Rosa doesn't want to learn of the Nose's fate climbing up a ladder to a bedroom window which she thought would reveal her husband but didn't, and coming down the quick, fatal way.

Here We Go

New day: I think about how to take care of the Gorgon vase.

No hurry. I've waited more than two thousand years, a few days aren't going to make any difference. I want to find a method that won't make Rosa seem careless or wanting in professionalism. Her hanging on to me is already getting her in trouble.

Tabatha comes around. She does the horror package on hearing about the Chin's sins.

"We live in confusing times," she asserts. Raw time-burster.

Tabatha's got enough concern for a nation. Tea and strategy. Merrythoughts and matchmaking. She tugs on her right earring (her sense of appropriate earwear hasn't improved, it codes the question: Who is the collector collector collector? She neither knows this nor senses it, nor would she understand it if it were explained to her): "Don't tell me you don't want to meet him. Verbalize me through this."

"An arrangement like this won't work," Rosa insists. "You've been a star, and I'll never be able to repay you, but this is a dead-end. If I give up, then maybe something will happen."

"I think you should meet him."

"Why?"

"Because you do have something in common."

"What?"

"He said the same thing."

Rosa doesn't have the fight left to protest. She agrees to a drink with Tabatha's discovery. One drink and farewell.

"Who was the guy you were talking to so intently at your party?" Rosa asks as Tabatha is leaving. "It looked as if you

175

were getting on very well. I have the feeling I've seen him somewhere before."

"Yes, you have. You probably didn't recognize him without the knife."

"You're not serious."

"He phoned up, offering to sell me back my address book, and we got talking."

"I'm in no position to say anything," Rosa concludes.

"It's working so far," says Tabatha. "To be frank, it's working very, very well in some senses."

"So what's not working very well?"

"He's extremely social. His friends spend a lot of time at my place."

I am placed in the safe Rosa has acquired.

It is old, ugly, not very large, but it is extremely heavy, making theft not impossible but exceedingly hard work. I am placed in the safe with the Gorgon vase. Humiliation and temptation on an alpine scale. Double humiliation and temptation on an alpine scale, since I am turned upside down and fitted on top of the Gorgon. I consider a protest. This is asking a lot of me.

I remain in this position for several hours. Nikki enters the flat with some people. Banal conversation. Rosa returns, sinks into her bed, but leaves me embracing the Gorgon. Her meeting was satisfactory since she prefers the company of the memory to any repast from my past.

The next morning, she leaves for Amsterdam to deal with a frieze and some Djenne and Luba figures—without saying good-bye. She is to be absent for three days. Nikki has some visitors—banal conversation.

Marius appears.

Nikki suggests that his fire extinguisher should be checked: They often fail to deliver in a crisis. Marius is swaying around in rage. He wants to know where I and the Gorgon are. Nikki says that Rosa has gone abroad and mentioned something about selling a bowl. Marius has difficulty breathing. Rosa wouldn't say anything about her journey, Nikki says, which made her suspicious. The chauffeur is summoned to provide Marius with a cylinder of oxygen. As he sucks deeply on that gas, Nikki explains that for five hundred up front she can tip him off about Rosa's activities. The wallet goes into action.

"Your judgement's shit, Marius. You trust the wrong people."

After Marius departs, the tumblers are unsuccessfully worked by Nikki. In the safe, I invent two hundred and one ways of smashing a Gorgon vase.

Rosa returns—without saying hello. Much telephoning. Much weighing up of perfumes. Later that evening, she returns accompanied. Shallow conversation.

The safe is opened.

"This is the sort of thing I do," Rosa says. Curly (Three Thousand Four Hundred and Seventy-Five), standing behind Rosa, does take the trouble to look at us, but his hands are already sneaking up to capture Rosa's breasts. A judicious ramble, she is a woman who will be undone by this. There was no real need to show Curly the contents of the safe, which is, of course, residing in Rosa's bedroom.

He rolls her breasts until there is no doubt as to where he will be spending the night, accomplished in sixteen seconds.

"I hope you don't mind," he says, undoing his shirt, unleashing a stocky chest and a smug right bicep on which is tattooed a rose and the name Rosa. "So it's presumptuous, but I have a feeling things are going to work out. I like to gamble, but I don't like to lose."

Having seen seduction performed four hundred thousand

nine hundred and eighty-one times, I have to concede that Curly is a whirly skinmaster. His confederates: wildness and mildness, best best breast-handling. Rose is overturned, not that she needed much in the way of a push. She unhooks her earrings (betokening a lone swimmer in a bright blue swimming pool swimming awkwardly to the side because he is holding aloft a soggy bumblebee, rescued from the tyranny of the water, on his right index finger) and puts them on the bedside table.

They turn off the light, but I can see anyway.

Curly runs a finger down the side of her face as if gently shaving her cheek. Nothing is said. The only sounds are those of collapsing clothes and panting. Rosa's nipples stretched out like baseball bats; his teeth turn into a harsh fun jailer for them.

Her eyes are nothing but white, and Rosa probably no longer knows her name. She offers him her neck, her lifeblood. Invisibly, inaudibly, undetectably, elephants who have lost all their elephantness except for their force now enter and press the two bodies together.

He removes Rosa's last piece of clothing. Rosa, managing to raise her bottom a fraction to aid him before blindfolding herself with her right arm in the international gesture: I'm steamrollered.

Curly's prong is burly; thick as the conger eel with the earring; all in all, I must say the quality most groaned for by women. Curly pulls at the inside of Rosa's thighs with his lips and faces the town of taste. But no direct assault. First, he flips her over and his tongue glides steadily up and down spine valley. His tongue leaves her back and moves decisively into her rear, his thumbs open her cheeks as if they're a book. His tongue carousels around as Rosa sprinkles the room with ooooooos, illustrating another example of nature's sense of humor and extravagance (such as snakes with enough venom to kill a village), those exciters buried in such an unsalubrious location.

Two fingers then play swimmer's legs in the main channel. Rosa has no more room for readiness, Curly raises himself ready to wobble her until she speaks Sumerian.

But he desists, and an uncleansable sadness ripples out on his face.

An ineffable one. He is motionless while the sadness permeates everything. He gets up. Rosa is spinning. She assumes he is looking for something in his clothes or carrying out some other trifling preliminary. She purrs as Curly, with considerable stealth and speed, puts his clothes back on and leaves.

Rosa emits a series of inquiring and then false plaintive noises. After a couple of minutes she goes to see if he is hiding somewhere in the kitchen. She struggles momentarily against despair before sagging into genuine plaintive noises and tear making.

I have to admit I have nothing on file as iguana as this. It is upsetting, and Rosa will torment herself trying to find a rule when there isn't one. Nikki is unlucky to be out; a desperate need to cling wracks Rosa.

"I don't want to be like this. I don't think I'm better than anyone else. I'm willing to work, I'm willing to fight. I've worked and I've fought and I don't mind that, as long as there's something to fight for, I'm willing to fight as hard as you can—as long as there's something. You have standards; you either end up hating everyone else and being on your own, or if you stoop you end up hating yourself; is that the choice? Confusing times."

She goes to the window. In the night, homes like flickering fireflies, the embers of the city.

"I know you're out there. I'm not so arrogant to think I'm that strange. But how do I find you?"

Cup of Tea: Thirty-One

"I don't understand, I keep on trying to see if it was something I said or did but all I was doing was lying there, moaning gratefully."

"Perhaps you weren't moaning in the right way," says Lettuce, unearthing a packet of chocolate raisins Rosa had hidden under some magazines. It is clear that this amity is a bit of a calamity for Rosa, but many friendships have a cockroachlike ability to survive despite having little to recommend them.

"What's the right way?"

"I don't know. I'm just trying to be helpful. It's never happened to me. Or anyone I know of. You're sure he wasn't married and, I know this sounds unlikely, he had a pang of conscience? These are fattening, aren't they?"

"He wasn't married. He doesn't have a girlfriend. He's just got back from six months in the Antarctic, fiddling with glaciers. We discussed how terrible it was for him to separate from his previous girlfriend. He should have been, by any standard, dying for it. He had my name tattooed on his arm. We talked about the future, and you know how popular that subject is with men."

Of course, but what Rosa doesn't appreciate is that the tattoo was not new. By my estimation, it was seven years old.

"Well, you know, perhaps women . . ."

"You could have used it as an ice pick. Something was exciting him and I don't think it was the potpourri."

"Maybe it wasn't meant to be."

"Well, that's pretty profound. Obviously something's

180

wrong. I wouldn't mind if I could just understand what it is. We got on ridiculously well. I felt as if I had known him for years. We liked the same books. The same films. The same music. His favorite food is Chinese. I really thought Tabatha had delivered the goods. It was almost as if he were hired to be perfect."

"Maybe he just gets his kicks warming up women."

"What's this?" says Nikki, walking in naked and giving Lettuce a long look.

"The disaster."

"Oh, that. You can never tell," says Nikki, scratching her left buttock richly. "I had a worse one. This Greek chef followed me home from the supermarket. He had a winning line: 'I bang your brains out, then I cook you something delicious with whatever is in the fridge.' He wasn't good-looking, but he was persistent and there wasn't much on television, so I thought, why not? For one evening, they're all pretty much the same.

"So I'm lying there with my ankles in my ears when he starts looking at me strangely and I think, Oh no, something's not right, have I shaved my armpits lately? Then, wait for this, he produces a sawed-off shotgun. We're both stark naked, he's got his dick in one hand, the shotgun in the other—and I like to think of myself as broadminded and non-judgemental, but I'm worried because he looks loopy. I say, 'Spiros, whatever it is you want, you know I'd love to do it for you, there's no need for the gun.' He stares at me like I'm a piece of slime with the heads of three former U.S. presidents. He raises the shotgun and I tell you that was quite a split-second, but he puts it in his mouth and pulls the trigger."

"Why did he do that?" asks Lettuce.

"I don't know. I would have liked to have asked him, but unfortunately he didn't really have a head anymore, not in any meaningful sense. You can't imagine how much I wished I'd just said no or washed my hair instead. Someone blows their brains all over your flat, do you think the insurance'll pay that? Not that I had any. Not to mention that I threw up all over the bits of the flat that weren't covered in bits of Greek. And you can imagine what fun I had with the police. 'No, I've no idea who he is. Where he lives. Where he works. I met him an hour ago, we came back to my place and instead of a florida he fancied blowing his brains out.' Lovely, that was."

Too true, Nikki, the truth is rarely needed. Philosophers. Scientists. Detectives. Teachers. Mothers. They praise the truth. What is really useful is better lies. The truth is hardly ever advantageous. The executed man about to go out to the gallows doesn't want to hear that it's all well-oiled; when his wife visits him, he wants to hear that there will be a pardon, but it will only be announced at the last second when he is hooded and in position, so that is what she says although she knows everyone's fighting over the best seats.

I first heard this formulation when I was in a wagon going over the Alps; the wheels slipped and half the wagon veered off into the picturesque abyss. The wagoneers sat motionless, afraid that any movement would precipitate an instantaneous tumble down to the rocks waiting patiently hundreds of feet below. The younger one looked back cautiously: "Half the wagon's off the edge." "What did you say that for?" reprimanded the elder. "We don't need to hear that. What we need is better lies."

"Such as?"

"I don't know what they are. I just know we need them. Do something."

The boy closed his eyes.

That was a nasty fall. It took me a while to pick up the

pieces and reconstitute myself. I think the idea-infested string bean on the Mop's boat had the same outlook. "You mustn't say we're sinking. It is rather that the sea is rising, rising everywhere, and all humanity shares our misfortune."

"It is depressing," says Lettuce, digging the last raisin out of the packet. "I've only seen one couple that managed to stay together, where I grew up. He ran the ferry, a rowboat; he must have been about seventy then. Storms, blizzards, Christmas Day he was there. He was really ugly and his wife's face looked as if it had been trodden on by an elephant. They were together because there was no one uglier. They were sickeningly poor but incredibly happy. No one ever saw them grumbling or even ill. Everyone talked about them a lot: She had this mustache, and he always said that the secret of their happiness was he enjoyed chewing her mustache in bed. People found this amazing, but I think the reason this went around and around was that it annoyed everyone that they were so happy."

When, in bed, Rosa comes to me to put on her hands what can I give her but . . .

Mustache Chewers of the Past and Their Painters

"He loves chewing it in bed," said the model. Lucas nodded.

My collector was a painter and a collector of antiquities as far as his means would allow. He worked hard and used white. A lot. He had bought a lot of it, cheap. Lucas's style didn't really fit in for 1440 in Venice; they liked it straight, but he would have been adored at Thera, and maybe one collector in Egypt who'd been dead for two thousand years would have taken to him. Now of course everyone goes for the white splash. The most important thing for any career:

183

Get born at the right time. Lucas's father was a brewer who, being boring, had found no problems with working hard all his life and had given Lucas five years to make money out of painting.

As Lucas was painting a creation myth with the aid of the spherical model (the mustache was of no interest to him at all), four years eleven months had elapsed and there had been a letter from his father telling him to come back or starve.

Lucas had done some good paintings (and I know what I'm talking about), but he hadn't sold any: No one was willing to commission work from him, and the few murals he had done gratis had been whitewashed. Nevertheless, this was an age of sweeping accomplishments; men held that no area of learning or skill should be strange to them. His greatest achievements had been in exterminating his detractors.

The abbot of the monastery who had refused his offer of a free Annunciation died when Lucas smeared the nipples of his favorite prostitute with cyanide.

Another who had animadverted on his picture of Jesus upon the water, Lucas dropped into the middle of the Adriatic.

"How does the sea look now? Can you see the white? Are you sure about that? You're not just saying this because you're drowning?"

"Yes, yes, no," said the man, though you might wonder if he was telling the truth since this was a few minutes past midnight.

"What sort of white do you see, and be careful how you answer this. I'm testing you."

"A wonderful white, just like the white you used in that painting which I didn't (splutter, splutter) understand because I had been too long away from the sea to recognize its true nature."

"Glad you agree with me," said Lucas, "I knew I could make you see reason." Lucas then rowed off, while the protestor tried to follow, without much success since his hands were tied behind his back, with heavy bindings that were soaking up water and made buoyancy contentious.

"You can't leave me," said the critic, "you're a priest."

"Yes, you're right, this is very wrong," Lucas replied. "But peculiarly—I don't know how closely you have studied the Church's teachings—God is considered to have this forgiving nature, so a few moments before I die, I'll confess manfully and crave divine indulgence. I'll give your favorite prostitute a visit for you."

But the prospect of his funds drying up preoccupied Lucas. We embarked on a ship, Lucas carefully carrying me and a dud Gorgon on board. Then he disappeared and returned with two toughs who were carrying a bulging blanket, tied up. This was down in the bowels of the ship, where even the toughs reeled from the stench. Their load was manacled there with little protest since he was clearly drugged. Gradually he recovered and started shrieking. Lucas reappeared.

"So, how are you? Are the dead rats entirely to your satisfaction?"

"Let me go at once. I could have you executed for this."

"Yes, you could, except you're manacled in a ship which is setting sail, and you're signally fucked. Now there's something I want to ask you: Do you still think that my picture of the gathering of angels is rubbish?"

"Yes." The man was brave.

"So you have no regrets about ruining my chances with the Doge and scuppering my career?"

185

"No."

"I see. Would your objection lie in the technique I employed?"

"Yes. Precisely." A dead rat bobbed affectionately next to him.

"Well, here's the situation, naturally everyone is entitled to their opinion; they are also entitled to die slowly by painful increments in the hold of this ship. I have here the work in question. I also have a canvas and paints. Most men can survive for weeks without food. I'm not a completely unforgiving man. If you make a perfect copy of my painting, which obviously shouldn't be so difficult since my skills are so weak, you can join us up in the fresh air and food. You can probably last a while if you eat some of the rats. On the other hand, they might eat you."

"Where's the Captain?"

"He's got other problems."

"But it's pitch dark here."

"Well . . . yes."

He foamed for a day, but then he started painting when he realized that the crew only came down to laugh at him. By the time we got to the Straits of Gibraltar, his copies were getting close. But no one was paying much attention. The Captain summoned the crew to listen.

"You think we're going to Bordeaux to deliver spices—well, we're not. We take on supplies and sail for Cathay."

"No, we're not," exclaimed the crew, mutinying in unison.

"What about the owners?" said one.

"They don't know," said the Captain. "Come on lads, think of the glory and the riches."

"No."

"All right," said the Captain, "who's the hardest man here?"

186

A long-haired ape sauntered up. "Everyone knows it's me."

"You don't want to go to Cathay?"

"No."

The Captain pulls out a Monk's gun and shoots him in the face, a novelty at that time. The ape goes overboard. Appreciation for innovative violence.

"I hope that settles that. Anyone wants to see how it works again, I'm happy to oblige. You know Pietro," he says, indicating a dauntingly large man with an axe in each hand. "He believes the people in Cathay are plotting to kill him so he has to get there to kill them first. He won't like it if anyone interferes. And you know the priest, he's an artist; he'll be painting the wonders of the new lands. He's also shifty, a superb poisoner, and doesn't just use his knife to cut his bread. He's someone else who, along with my brother Argentino, wants to get to Cathay, so don't think about further discussion. Think of the fame you will gain. Is there a man here who doesn't want fame?"

"Yes," said one fellow.

"Why not?"

"Because it's not much use when you're dead, and not that much use when you're alive; it doesn't make you happy."

"What about gold then, fellow? Don't you want that?"

"No."

"Why the devil not?"

"Because money doesn't make you happy. I will be glad to list the things that bring happiness if you care to listen."

"No. I hope you enjoy the voyage anyway and you can remind us about that when we return to Venice like kings, one and all. Remember when a man built the first boat, everyone stood on the shore and said, 'What's the good of that? Why not walk?' Someone has to be first."

187

The adviser in the hold survived another week. "It's a shame—his work was becoming quite intriguing toward the end," Lucas noted. "The contrasts in particular. I might steal those."

Weeks out, the crew got odd. The cook jumped overboard because the Captain always wanted his fish with basil. Every evening. Every lunch. Even for breakfast or a snack. Fish, whatever was caught, with basil.

"Wouldn't you like it with lemon, or garlic?"

"No."

"It's unbelievably good with almonds."

"No. With basil."

"The sauce with peppers is so good, several men died fighting over it."

"With basil."

"My fish with onion and spinach is considered the best thing I do."

"Basil."

The cook jumped in the night; in the morning, there was no one to cook the fish with basil, though he had left instructions. Eight hours later, a figure was spotted in the water. The cook.

"It's the cook, Captain."

"It can't be the cook," declared the Captain, peering down at the swimmer. "The cook jumped yesterday—he couldn't have swum this far in front of us. It stands to reason this is a demon in a remarkable likeness, or a she-dragon in disguise, knowing that I have eaten enough basil as a defense against it, trying to get on board to persuade me to stop eating basil."

"Perhaps," said the first mate, "but of course we all believe the world is round."

"So?"

"Well," said the first mate, "if it is round, we could have

sailed down to a point where we're so near the pole that we might have caught up with the cook who fell overboard last night." It was a nice try.

The Captain leaned overboard.

"Who are you?"

"I am the cook. Who are you?"

"I'm the Captain. Why do you ask?"

"Why are you asking who I am?"

"Because I suspect that you are a transformed she-dragon trying to get on board to persuade me to stop eating basil."

"Very prudent of you," said the cook, "but actually, if I were a she-dragon I could think of better things to do than splashing around in the water. I suspect you are a ship of skillfully transformed devils who look just like my former shipmates in order to lure me on board and to lead me to damnation."

"Just what I would expect a she-dragon to say."

"Or," said the cook.

"Or?"

"Or, you are my former shipmates, but you are a laughably bad navigator and you've gone in a circle."

"Exactly what a she-dragon would say."

"What she-dragon, wanting to get on board, would insult you by calling you the most incompetent captain in Christendom?"

"A she-dragon would insult me precisely in that fashion so it would look as if she didn't want to get on board."

"You don't suppose there's any chance of a great fish coming up and eating this she-dragon?" asked Lucas, holding his sketch pad. "I've always wanted to do a Jonah and the Whale."

"Would a she-dragon also call you a hairy ape with beards growing out of his ears?"

189

"Probably."

"Look, I'm getting bored. Either pick me up or tell me how to sink. I've forgotten."

"You're dying to get on board."

"No, I'm not. I suppose I'll get to see you tomorrow when you'll be back around."

"Sink the she-dragon," the Captain ordered, as they threw holy relics that hadn't been pulling their weight at the bobbing head.

They sailed for three weeks, without sight of land. Soon it became clear to the crew that there was no point in even thinking about mutinying because they couldn't make it back, and if they were in charge, they'd have to forgo the pleasure of hatred. They had to go forward.

Then Lucas started seeing the future. "I've seen the future," said Lucas to the Captain.

"What have you seen?"

"Sea," said Lucas.

"Anything else?"

"No, just sea."

"In that case," remarked the Captain, "I think I might be seeing the future, too. Is it rather wavy, wet, gray?"

"You don't believe me, do you?" said Lucas. "I know what the sea's going to be like tomorrow at this time."

"That's nice," said the Captain, "but we're all going to find out after twenty-four hourglasses anyway, I don't see how you're going to turn this gift of yours into a profitable sideline."

"Fine. I'll paint the sea as it will be tomorrow."

So he painted assiduously, the waves as they would be and the clouds bunched like fuds above the suds.

The crew was astonished the following day to discover it was just as Lucas had painted, though Lucas maintained he had done the clouds with more vim than God. He sat down and painted the sea for the next day, a gray sea and clouds in the shape of icy reptiles. Sure enough, the next day the painting was a perfect match for the weather. The crew was stunned. "Are we going to reach land?" they asked Lucas. "Yes," he said, "I can see more and more. We'll reach land in six days' time." He played a lot of dice in the meantime and won all the money any of them had hoped to return with.

"I went to an old wise woman in Portugal who was blind and toothless but who'd suck you and tell you your fortune. She was famed for her accuracy," the Captain reminisced.

"What did she say, 'Mmmmmggg, mmgghhh, mmmmmbbb-gggg'?" suggested Lucas.

"No, she told me my fortune afterward."

"So what did she say?"

"I don't know. I don't speak Portuguese. I did get something about my going on a long voyage. But who wants to know the future? You wouldn't bother leaving the harbor." His toothache was bothering him.

They sighted land as foretold and wanted to land but they were naked because all their clothes had been put over the side to be washed. Pietro had threaded all the clothes onto a rope and then hoisted it over the side to let the waves do the work; he had failed to secure the rope properly; if it had been anyone else but Pietro, the remonstrating would have been bitter.

"We're saved," chimed the crew as they waded ashore without any clothes. Only Pietro was left on the ship.

"There's a river just beyond the hill, and you'll find some tempting fruit trees on the right," said Lucas. "Now if you'll excuse me, I have some business to attend to." So saying, he strolled over to some trees by the beach and painted a picture of himself hanging from a bough, portrait of the artist as a

corpse in a copse, a unique enterprise as far as I know, with a
squirrel climbing a falling branch that had dropped off the
same tree.

"Yes, I can see it all now," he said, and then hanged himself. A minute later the squirrel plummeted. So Lucas wasn't
around when the indigenes arrived, sorely displeased about
their fruit trees being depleted. The crew was unarmed since
the Captain hadn't allowed them any weapons. The indigenes
were amused by these strange savages who weren't civilized
enough to wear clothes or interesting makeup or to have
invented weapons; they found the screaming satisfactory
though it was a pity they had no common ground linguisti-
cally since they missed out on the details of the begging for
mercy. There was some debate as to whether the bare-arsed
intruders were human or merely some bizarre new ape. The
Captain was the only one to escape, rowing back with me and
sacks of fruit to Pietro, who was sharpening his axes.

We sailed on.

And on.

And on.

I'm quite good at the patience, but this was a heinous
voyage. The Captain and Pietro were soon reduced to talking
only a couple of times a day; a painted division line runs
down the center of the ship. They take turns on the rudder.
The lodestone is out for the count. They don't seem to
understand stars, and even the rising of the sun doesn't help
them much.

There are huge barrels on the deck to collect rainwater.
They drop a net to fish. God help any seabirds that come
near. The basil plants grow, a number in me and in what is
left of the Gorgon vase. The many barrels of dried fruit, nuts,
and honey are devoured. The two men spend the time
insulting each other, the only rule being that an insult cannot

be repeated in the same day. This leads to a lot of bickering and abuse outside the official insult joust itself. They also spend a lot of time arguing over who was the biggest arsehole they've ever met. A barber in Genoa makes a strong showing.

This went on for a year and a half; we didn't sight land.

Or rather, they didn't. I spotted land masses forty, fifty, sixty miles away, but I didn't say anything. Several times we passed close to land, but it was dark or foggy. Twice we passed close to land but they didn't notice because they were furiously swearing at each other. They saw a few distant ships that looked familiar. Travel doesn't necessarily broaden the mind.

They wouldn't have withstood the privation if it hadn't been for two deliveries of foodstuffs. The first was a polar bear on a small disk of ice which must have once been a mighty ice floe; the bear was hungry and irked but it didn't stand a chance against Pietro, who was not fooled by the natives of Cathay hiding in a fur coat. The second was a dugout adrift, filled with pineapples. The distribution of the pineapples was another bitter subject of altercation for the remainder of the voyage.

Finally, the ship went aground one night and its timbers disintegrated on contact.

They climbed down, almost unable to walk. They staggered on till they saw a man plowing a field. "Don't hit him until I've asked a few questions," said the Captain.

"We have come from Venice, to find Christians and to do business," said the Captain, speaking very slooooowly. I'm surprised the plowman didn't just run; they made roughness smooth.

"I'm a plowman, shipman, not an imbecile. There's no need to speak slowly."

"How do you manage to speak our tongue so well?"

"How do you?"

He didn't get any further because Pietro kicked him in the stomach. "One down. Amazing. They've learned how to speak our language for the invasion," he commented, before dying of exhaustion.

The Captain walked on to the city, which strongly reminded him of Venice, as it was Venice. Nearly two years after they had left and invectively circumnavigated the globe, they landed twelve miles away from it. The Captain occupied himself before he died in poverty by asking for directions to the Great Cane or by asking for alms to get back to Venice so he could tell them about Cathay and how men are much the same everywhere.

Rosa isn't satisfied with this. I give her the good Godding guide and I decide to smorgasbord some more of her past.

Rosa goes into a pub. She hates pubs, but she is thirsty after having a curry with Marius.

"I don't like Indian food, Marius."

"You haven't eaten proper Indian food," says Marius.

"I'd really prefer anything but Indian."

"No, no, you don't mean that, you don't know what you're talking about," says Marius. The food is distasteful, the restaurant expensive. "I won't insult you by offering to pay for you," says Marius.

Driven by thirst, she orders an orange juice. It is afternoon, quiet. The bartender disappears for a moment, and just then a man comes up and asks her for change because he's making a phone call. When he returns he sits next to her and asks in a friendly manner if he can buy her a drink. She had been thinking of leaving, but the curry is not entirely slaked.

They talk without effort; the words fall like ripe fruit. After half an hour, it occurs to her that she has never got on so well with anyone in her life. She tries not to panic. It's like meeting an old friend. A reunion with no previous union, witty but not showing off, no stunts, no coronation parade. Gentlemanly, yet thrusting. She starts the rundown on the catches: Partnered? Spliced? Shirt lifter? Terminally ill? About to be gunned down? Dick lost in tragic childhood accident with lawnmower?

So when he says, "I'd ask you out, but I'm emigrating to Australia early tomorrow morning," she is almost pleased because she saw the hitch in hitching coming. Rosa can't see (although she likes it), but I can that he is a vaulter who will jump breezily into any opportunity, so he really must be behind in his packing.

She was prepared and avoids visible crestfalling; she ignores the despair nipping at her ankles. Rosa smiles and asks if he has an address in Australia since she had been thinking of booking her holiday there. He looks surprised but jots down an address on a coaster.

He makes wildlife films. Ardently, he talks of djintamoongas and wopilkaras. Rosa emphasizes that she's very keen to go to Australia and wouldn't it be funny if they met up there? Rosa notices that she's hoping he might simply brazenly suggest pleasure at the nearest convenient location, but she also knows that it's one of the steady wormwoods

195

that men who brazenly suggest pleasure are the ones with whom you have no inclination to have brazen or indeed any sort of pleasure, while those whom you quite fancied brazen pleasure with never offered it. "I must go and pack," he said. She wondered about offering to help fold shirts but concluded it would be too pathetic. She opted for the brave, fellatious face and a heart-rending desire to bite his buttocks as he walked out.

She tried convincing herself that he wasn't so irresistible, but thinking of him made warm shivers run through; he was a true hanger for her love. She carefully took the address out of her purse twice on the way home to make sure it was there, gratified by its ink, elated to see her future suspended in writing. She even thought about copying it down somewhere else, but she didn't have a pen. Then she spent the rest of the journey musing on whether good wedding dresses were available in Australia. It was a challenge but one she would rise to.

Running herself a bath, she decided to study the address again as if that would bring happiness to pass, but she couldn't find her purse. It was gone. Lost. Swiped. Absconded. She dressed up again and rewalked her route. Three times. She inquired at lost-property offices.

She went out to Melbourne anyway. She only went to her hotel room to sleep, sitting in the most public of places, putting an ad in the local paper. Then putting in another one three days later when there had been no response, and one more the day before she left since she didn't have much else to do. She had been to all the places with animal connections as well as some museums, taking some hits from vases and objects, siphoning off some of their history.

Some fourteen months, an unemployed aid worker, and a blood-bank organizer later, she got a call from the police saying her purse had been recovered, the romantic Paraguayan pickpocket who had acquired it having kept it because of a photograph of Rosa he had described as "enchanting." If it had been a test, now she had passed; in a flap of her purse was the piece of paper with the address.

She flew out two days later and took a taxi from the airport to the address only to find a squat building with no hideaway entrances that was the Czech consulate. She tried all the other combinations of the number, perhaps it was 148 rather than 48, or 84, perhaps there was an avenue as well as a road, but to no avail. She did ring the bell at the consulate, though barely able to raise her arm under the deadening weight of disappointment that was camped on it, because she knew that if she didn't she'd only have to pay for a taxi later on when she decided to come back and do it. She explained whom she was looking for and the woman she talked to called the police.

She placed another small ad, unable to shake off the thought that if there were a worldwide competition for most difficulty in finding someone you get along with, at worst, she'd come in as runner-up. She sits in a sidewalk café, the Argentina, and surveys the menu; she looks at the newspaper and reads an item empathetically about a woman who has broken her left leg thirteen times, twice while it was still in plaster. The twelfth time she had been crossing the road when a car had roared up out of nowhere—she had enough time instinctively to turn her right side to meet the impact. She rolled over the top of the car and onto the road, where her left leg was crushed by a remaindered armored personnel carrier driven by an ice-cream vendor. She took to bed after that, doing work addressing envelopes, and not going out, remembering the warning of a gypsy who had told her a left leg was on the cards again, and to avoid soccer at all costs, which the woman found odd since she had never played the game, had never attended a match, and had no intention of doing so. She had chuckled at the prediction until her ceiling collapsed and her upstairs neighbor's filing cabinet, crammed with soccer programs, crashed down on her left leg, totaling her tibia. It would be all right if you knew it would be thirteen, Rosa reasons, if you were assured at the start, then you could count them down and get on with it. Maybe I will look back on my failures and see a number with some significance, twenty-three, the number of years I've lived. Perhaps one day Mr. Right will just come crashing through the ceiling into my bed.

The waiter comes up to her and tells her about the special.

"Iguana."

"What, fresh?"

"No, it's frozen. But it tastes great."

That night she pulls the sheet over her head, to hide from the world and to hide it. Her room is cheap but rich in misery: never-loved furniture, feel-bad curtains, antijoy bed. She's had a planetful. She lies there too depressed to do more than breathe. She planned to stay for a few weeks, but she gets a call from the auctioneeress telling her about a pair of earrings.

Ooooooff come the hands. Rosa has digested the good Godding guide.

"You're the only one who understands me," she sighs, hugging me.

Rosa goes to sleep.

The End

Rosa rises and finds her face waiting for her in the mirror. Nikki returns.

"I think there's a new neighbor," she says. "He's quite hunky." They hear thumping sounds from upstairs. "He's either hard on his furniture, or he likes his florida wild. If he carries on like that, he'll come through the ceiling."

Rosa pauses and reflects on this.

"Maybe you should put the house on the market. Might be a good way of finding young men about town." Nikki yawns. "I'm exhausted. There's very little worse than someone who thinks that because you're sleeping together, they're entitled to tell you their life story all night."

Rosa fills the pot.

"Tell me, Nikki, are you happy?"

Nikki is reluctant to speak about a subject that she regards as taboo; she is embarrassed by a question she sees as tactless.

"You move around so much. Are you looking for something, or are you trying to lose something?"

"I hadn't thought about it. Bit of both."

"Are you happy?"

"Yes. I suppose I am. If things aren't bad. You can't have it all, I know that now. I used to think you could. No, you can choose how you lose, you get some freedom. As long as your dissatisfaction is satisfactory."

Lettuce arrives to borrow a jacket and has a go at the new jar of pickled beetroot.

"How can they design things this way?"

"Can I fix you something to eat, Lettuce?" inquires Rosa.

"No. No, I'm not hungry."

"What about you, Nikki?"

"Not for me," she says, staring at Lettuce's knoll. "My toothache's bothering me."

One wonders with the potency of the dope why she can't cope.

Marius phones. He is worried about his collection.

"That was Marius. He's fretting about his pottery."

"I can understand that," says Lettuce, "I miss my teddy bears."

"Teddy bears?" Nikki polishes her teeth with her tongue.

"I used to have a collection of teddy bears. From the ones I had as a child to bears from all over the world. I had over two hundred."

"Two hundred?"

"Some of them were very small, mini-bears." She untubs some hummus and takes a big spoonful. "They marked my life. Bears I bought after exams. Bears I bought on my travels. Bears I got as birthday presents. A bear I got after an abortion. Bears in cars. Bears in submarines. Bears in biplanes. Bears snowboarding. Bears carrying hearts. Bears getting married. Bears in parliament. Bears in lederhosen. Bears in flying saucers. Bears with pencils up their ends."

"Dead pets," says Nikki. "So what happened?"

"I moved in with a teddy-bear hater," says Lettuce, coveting the mango chutney. The lid sighs off a treat. "He said they'd have to go. I argued but I thought this was it. I thought I could stick the bears away somewhere, but he insisted that I put them in the dustbin while he watched."

"Why did he dislike them so much?"

"I don't know. He just disapproved of teddy bears. He said they were evil. So I dropped the bag in and we went back inside. About an hour later I sneaked out to rescue them, but they'd already gone, because he must have sneaked out before me and dumped them somewhere else."

"So how long did it last?"

"Two days," says Rosa.

"Three," insists Lettuce, noticing after her insistence that it wasn't worth insisting. She is dropping mango chutney all

200

over the place in her agitation. "I spent days wandering around the municipal dump in the hope of finding the bags. I miss them; they supported me."

"When you say they supported you, you mean they didn't walk out on you?" interposes Nikki.

"Yes."

"I hope the florida was extraordinary."

"He felt that penetrative stuff was old-fashioned." She examines a tomato wearing a wig of mango chutney. "Perhaps I'm not saying this the right way."

"You probably are. So what did he go for?" She is really interested.

"I never found out."

"He got his kicks trashing bears." says Rosa, hiding some chocolates.

"No doubt about it," says Nikki. "Loveshit can harm your bears."

"Perhaps we shouldn't believe in it," Rosa reflects. "In my last year at school, someone suggested we all drive down to Brighton for the day. You know how it is when you're eighteen—you'll go to the other side of the world for a party or just to see if it's there. We decided to go on a Friday—I still remember it well because of triple Chemistry period. So I got up and waited for them to come and pick me up. And I waited and I waited. After a couple of hours I phoned up to see where they were. I was tempted just to go into school for the remaining half-day, but I thought they must have had a flat tire or some problem and they'd be along and they'd be annoyed if, after all that, I wouldn't be there. They didn't turn up because, of course, they'd gone to school. It was a joke, which I didn't find very funny then and I still don't."

"You must still be in touch with all your school friends," says Nikki.

"But I'm coming round to the view that a lot of life is like that. People tell you something, but it isn't so and are quite surprised that you took them seriously."

"Yes, my mother's like that," reflects Lettuce. "When I was depressed after my second abortion and I went to see her, and I just wanted to be hugged and pampered and told, Never mind, things'll get better, you wait and see—regular, simple motherlike things, even if she didn't mean them at all. 'Of course, you're depressed, you're right to be depressed, and it's going to get worse' was what she said. They should teach you the important things at school; the Battle of Hastings, that's not useful, or not the way it's taught. If they pointed out that life was all about getting your arse kicked by more successful, better-dressed people, that might be a help."

"Yeah, you're right," says Nikki, thoughtfully. "They don't teach the important things. I remember thinking that when I ended up in bed with my headmistress. There wasn't a class explaining that the finest moments of your life would be with your face jammed between someone's thighs."

"You went to bed with your headmistress?" marvels Lettuce. Perhaps Nikki is hoping to raise the salacity of the room, because if one lesson in life is sure, if you don't open the window the goose liver isn't going to fly into your mouth.

"All above board. I'd left school. Met at a club. Things happen. Quite an education."

Lettuce is unable to go on eating Rosa's hot-cross buns.

"Honestly," Rosa says, "do you know of a happy couple, or a couple who have been happy for more than a few months? I know of people who stay together because they can't be bothered to move out and they've found space in their partner's disgusting habits."

"No, it happens," says Nikki, the last one I would expect to defend the unturning. "One of the weirdest jobs I ever had.

This gent was dying of cancer, mid-forties, and he started to find a new man for his wife. What he did was put an ad in the paper; it wasn't 'new husband sought' or anything like that, it was some management position, he had his own company. So he interviewed dozens of men, weeded out the hopelessly wed, boring, the laughable, got a short list, and then a number of us were sent out to road-test them. Did they help us off with our coats, did they help us get off, did they listen politely to our stories, did they tell the truth? It was a big operation. I had this guy from Birmingham. You know how everyone always makes these jokes about Birmingham, about how dull people are there? How bloody right they are. Biscuit factory. He whittled it down to a short list of three, introduced them all to his wife the week before he died."

"Did she marry any of them?" asks Lettuce.

"That I don't know."

Lettuce lowers the level of the nut bowl. "I've never really liked pistachios," she says. "At the travel agent's I worked at just before my first nervous breakdown, all the men spent their time leering at women, but there was one guy who spent the whole time saying how much he looked forward to seeing his wife in the evening. They hardly ever went out, and they'd been married a couple of years. I thought that was sweet."

"So he would have taken the bullet?" inquires Nikki.

"Mmm?" says Lettuce, masticating a bean salad.

"Taken the bullet. That's what it's all about," says Nikki. "Risk everything for someone. How do you manage to stay so thin?" she asks Lettuce.

"By eating other people's food," Rosa answers. "Still you don't know in either of these cases whether it lasted. Three unhappy years of marriage can go kablooey just as easily as ten happy years. It might be the guy who was looking for a replacement was looking for a nonentity so that his wife wouldn't forget him."

"And I thought I was the cynical one," said Nikki.

"Why don't men stay anymore?" asks Lettuce, opening a tin of anchovies. "Anyone for an anchovy?" she inquires, as if this is why she opened the tin. "I mean, they used to roll over and fall asleep and then expect you to make them breakfast in the morning. They don't even do that anymore. They get up and you think they're going to the toilet but they're calling for a cab and they're gone."

"We live in degenerating times," says Rosa.

"Men go, the florida remains," remarks Nikki.

"I don't know, everyone I talk to complains," says Lettuce. "You open the magazines and the whining just floods out."

"That's because the happy keep quiet and probably have better things to do than to listen to you."

"You know about it sometimes," says Lettuce, "sometimes you're grouting the bathroom or looking out the window and you feel happy for no reason. I think that's because you've been hit by the ricochet of a great fuck between true lovers." She dives into the anchovies. "I was thinking about going on holiday, I need some color, but I don't want to go alone."

"I've never seen the point of taking a man on holiday myself," says Nikki. "It's like taking a kitchen sink with you. Unless you're absolutely sure where you're going hasn't got a kitchen sink. Another weird job I had was work for this couple. It has to be said they were willing to work at it. They'd been married ten years or so, and every year they'd arrange to go on holiday for two weeks. But they'd go separately. What they'd do was they'd agree on a place, say Venice. She'd go out on an earlier flight, and he'd follow but he wouldn't know where she'd be staying. She'd have a false name, new clothes, change of hairstyle, and he'd have the two weeks to track her down. They had very intricate rules, about how you were only allowed to spend so many hours at the hotel. But part of the game was they arranged temptations for each other, and at the end they had to guess what was set up and what wasn't."

"What was the point?"

"To oomph up the relationship. And if he didn't find her, he had to walk the dog every day, but if he found her, she had to walk the dog."

"But what was the point of the temptations?"

"Well, of course I assumed it was a call for kinkiness and I didn't mind—they were a nice couple—but I think it was designed to prevent them from actually doing anything, since they never knew whether it was a real overture or not. Complicated."

"Do you think the past's a comfort when you're in trouble?" asks Rosa.

"Depends on the trouble, and depends on the past." says Nikki.

"It's not only the sex," says Lettuce. "One of the things I enjoyed most was shopping for him. I used to love buying food I knew he liked. It was like feeding a dog; he'd get very excited."

"And trust, it's not even fidelity," says Rosa, "but the knowledge that you can count on them, that in a grave situation, when the city is burning down, they'd get off the French maid and look for you."

"Do you think there are three intelligent personable men sitting around a table wondering where we are?" speculates Lettuce.

"Not likely," says Nikki. "They'll be talking about football."

"What is football all about?" asks Lettuce.

"Football is precisely not about football. It has nothing to do with the spherical object that gets booted around," remarks Rosa.

Nikki withdraws to wash her hair (or more likely her arteries). Rosa shows Lettuce out. "I wish I could help you," Rosa says. "If there was a button I could push, I'd do it. Or even if it was something more. I'm not sure there's anything you can do to help anyone. I'm not sure you can even help yourself. I saw a squirrel today jumping from one tree to another, the branch it landed on snapped. So the squirrel was on this falling branch, clambering like mad, thinking it was doing something about it."

Her hands come ooooooon. I give her the City of Skiing Lizards.

Mr. Annihilator

The next morning, Rosa leaves to authenticate a Cycladic frying pan in Birmingham. She ponders whether or not to take me; she decides to leave me in the safe with the rubbish.

Fifteen minutes after she goes, the tumblers tumble. Nikki's grinning face appears. Judging from the correct sequence of numbers, she must have found the combination in Rosa's effects.

"You'll make a nice farewell present," she says.

It looks as if she's preparing the Big Clearout. The Gorgon is placed on the mantelpiece and I am left on the new table, while she goes for a good-bye shower. I consider this is a good moment to stretch over and give the Gorgon a nudge.

He comes in. The new door and the new locks just don't take their work seriously.

He's got long orange hair in spikes, as if he stuck a

number of large shocked orange starfishes on his head. Sunglasses, the fashionable disguise. A parrot-green suit. Gloves. You have to be either completely inconspicuous or so conspicuous no one will know you.

He carries a small bag from which he pulls a gun. He gives Nikki a welcoming smile as she comes out of the bathroom.

"I've got a message for you. Forgive me barging in on you like this." Nikki instantly considers the running-screaming routine but realizes this is instant death.

"Sit down. Relax." He's having fun. Nikki has wet hair and red underwear. "Your hand, please." He produces an inkpad and paper, takes her fingerprint, then compares it with a blow-up he has, using a photographer's eyeglass.

He takes out a list. "So, Magenta Scott? Blanche Rickenbauer? Candida Jones? Olive Frampton? Violet Nugent? You've got a colorful imagination, young lady. What shall I call you?"

"Anything you fancy."

"Nikki's up to date, isn't it? I like to be up to date."

"I'm sorry I didn't catch your name."

"They call me Mr. Annihilator."

"Are you telling me you haven't made that up?"

"More money. You can charge double with a name like that. Clients feel they're getting a service. If you have a name like Fred Bloggs, you're already down a few thousand. True, most of my clients are so stupid they don't know what it means, but it sounds right. Some of them can't even pronounce it, of course, they call me Ann. But you're a clever girl."

"What can I do for you, Mr. Annihilator?"

"Well, Nikki, you can die, compliantly, in a suicidal manner. Oh, I should say if you believe in that guff about keeping people talking, they see you as a person and they find it harder to kill you—I don't. Why don't you ask me how I got started?"

"How did you get started?"

"Strangled this fat bastard. Manchester United supporter. You know, people give you shit about how hard it is to kill people. It's not hard at all. More work for me, I suppose, I hardly touched him. Just a . . . little squeeze. Have you ever noticed how irritating fat people are? Weak necks. Anyway if you haven't found yourself doing a stretch for manslaughter, count yourself lucky."

"I'll bear that in mind."

"So I was sixteen, when I had my life ruined by this bastard with a weak neck. Okay, it wasn't all bad; I had the best sex of my life inside, and by the time I got out, I had my qualifications in forensic science. Sold my story to a newspaper. Go back home, wondering what to do, when one of the neighbors asks me to bump off his business partner. Accountant. I got him to poke an inflatable woman and then leave a suicide note explaining he was ending it all because of how sordid his life had become. Never looked back."

He takes out a bunch of hairs. "I collect them," he says and spreads them over the room. "I love giving the forensic boys work. Hairs from all over the world. Dab of blood. From an iguana. They'll love it. 'So what was the iguana doing there?' I'll even take some of yours."

He sets down an empty bottle. "One I found earlier in a garbage can around the corner. I don't think they'll investigate, but you don't get to the top by making things easy. Put some of this under your nails. You leave no evidence, every moron knows that, but you also leave antievidence. This is one of my favorites," he says, producing a pint glass. "The head of the Met's forensic division drinks in my local pub. I

208

love discussing the cases and collecting his glasses. One day they'll turn up in an investigation.

"Now," he says. "Listen to this." He sticks a video into the new player.

"Shiner?" inquires Nikki.

A face appears. He doesn't say much. He curses apoplectically for five minutes, till he is struggling for breath and his voice is ripped; even with the volume turned down, it is deafening.

"You're supposed to respond," Annihilator says, switching on a pocket tape recorder.

Nikki clears her throat. "Shiner. I faked every orgasm. And you have the smallest willy I've ever seen, and I've seen a few." She stops. No insult is too old to work. He gives a quizzical look as if she's sure that's it. Then he turns off the recorder. "Guff this stuff, but you get extra," he says, packing away the tape. "He does look like a real turd," he says.

"Yeah, he'll know I'm trying to get to him, but it'll still get to him. I can't offer you some money?"

"Got any?"

"I could get some."

"No, let's not waste time. I always get this, to be honest; if you did happen to have some serious money lying around, I'd just say thanks and carry on as usual. You'd only be buying yourself a few seconds. The accountants all do that. They go to their stash and think I'm just going to go away. That's the thing about this job—you'd think you'd get to meet some interesting people, but most of my work: husbands and wives. Business partners, one of whom wants all the custard. They all know about me, but they're not going to shop me because one day they might want a little service. Every time you read about some accountant wanking himself to death with a plastic bag over his head or a bit of fruit in his mouth, that's me. Or at least some of them. The police are too busy laughing to do any serious work. I've even done a Chief Constable, at the request of the Assistant Chief Constable. The widows don't want any fuss. They don't want discussions about did he wank himself to death or *not*. You shouldn't worry about people like me; you should worry about those close to you."

"If I can't offer you money, perhaps I can offer you something else."

"No, I think not. It complicates things, and I don't mean to be personal but I think you're past your best, your bum's getting lumpy. I'm sure you could doll yourself up and wiggle about in a fun way, but I'll pass. Besides, women in your position often do strange things. Someone I knew was out on a job, took up the offer of a sexual favor, had his dick bitten off."

"The whole thing?"

"Enough to make an enormous difference to his life. And he ended up with six years for attempted murder. Can you imagine spending six years inside with everyone calling you Dickless? Now, why's this Shiner stumping up bigtime to have us meet? Were you his wrongdoing woman?"

"Sort of. We did have a brief relationship. And it was brief—we're talking under a minute every time. I suspect what upset him most was my having a romantic interlude with his wife."

"That upset him? Most men would cough up big for an arrangement like that. Wouldn't you let him join in?"

"I don't think he wanted to. It didn't do anything for him, and he was also pissed off because his wife told him that I had more staying power. But I'd guess the main reason you're here is there was something else she enjoyed informing him about."

"What's that?"

"I was born a Nicholas not a Nicola."

Annihilator falls off his chair. He laughs until he cries. Nikki could be lying. But she could be telling the truth. I can't tell on this one.

"That's bad luck, too. Most of the accountants I deal with would get off on that. Dear, oh dear. I haven't had a laugh like this for a long time. I do enjoy these talks. Conversation's a much undervalued commodity. Okay, so here's what we do. You're going to eat a lot of sleeping pills in a few minutes."

"What if I don't want to?"

"Then I shoot you. And if I have to shoot you, I don't have to make it painless. Take it from me, the pills are fine."

"And you think that won't be suspicious?"

"Haven't you seen what happens at inquests? All right, there are obvious ones, bankrupts, broken hearts, etcetera, but there are so many where the family and friends line up to say, 'We saw her the day before. She was cheerful. Didn't have a care in the world.' That's what they'll say about you."

"I had someone try and kill me the other week."

"You're good at making friends, aren't you? But don't you see, that'll make it all the more convincing. How ironic, people will say, she survived that only to top herself. People love irony. They can't get enough."

"I should warn you," says Nikki, raising her voice slightly. "I have a guardian angel, who doesn't like people killing me."

"Well, he should speak up then, shouldn't he?" He cups his ear attentively. I wonder if the bug that Lump put in the electrical socket behind the pile of magazines is still working. Or if she is. "Looks like Guardian Angel: nil. Annihilator: one. True, it is outrageous that I've been allowed to get away

211

with all this. What does that say? Okay, here's my funny five minutes: I want you to take off your knickers, do a head-stand, and we'll pretend you're a vase, and I'll stick a flower into your puss."

Having done much weirder things, Nikki complies and neatly balances on her head and shoulders. Annihilator takes a daffodil from the crappy vase and works it into Nikki.

"This is the bit I like best, where people do anything, absolutely anything to live for a few minutes longer. What I want to ask: Is it really worth it? You've got a close-up view of some shitty carpet, and you must be getting uncomfortable. I mean if some turd with outrageous orange hair came in and told me to crawl, I'd tell him to fuck off."

"I bet you wouldn't. Give me the gun."

"How's the carpet?"

"Okay. Better than living in Market Harborough."

"Why don't you tell me about your most outlandish sexual experience?" prompts Annihilator.

We're going to be here all day. It probably isn't her most outlandish experience.

"I had a family once. In Tunisia. Sister. Brother. Mother. Father. Aunt. Uncle. Cousins. I was thinking about the grand-father, 'cause he was in good shape, to complete the set. But they did have some relatives in another town. Where do you draw the line?"

"That's not bad. Could you give me some more detail to make my future re-creations of the scene more intense?"

"They all said, 'Don't tell anyone. I don't normally do this sort of thing.' "

"Interesting, but not especially juicy. What about life itself? Is there anything you've learned that's really impor-tant you want to pass on?"

"Avoid orange-headed men with guns."

"You're being flippant. How can you be flippant? I'm trying to have a serious discussion here. What about regrets, do you have any?"

"No, I made a point of no regrets. Mistakes but no regrets."

"You should have a few regrets. Gives you something to think about."

"What's your regret?"

"Didn't shoot two pricks. I was going home from a job that had gone pear-shaped, I'd had to shoot the guy. I walk in and say, 'Get on the floor.' He says, 'That's not a real gun.' I say it is. He comes at me with a pineapple. It hurts. So I shoot him. Then I'm walking down the road and these two turds come up to me and ask me for my money. One was about fifteen. Broad daylight, and there's this security camera. I had the gun—I could have shot them, one between the eyes each, and strolled on. But I thought, It's not worth the trouble. So I give them the money. Do they bugger off? No. Turd number one produces a flick knife; you know, it had probably taken him an hour to work out how to open it, and he says, 'Lick my boots.' This police car crawls by, can you believe it? I'm thinking, I should have plugged them, but once you've made the decision, you have to stick to it. It occurs to me maybe someone's looking out a window and sees the knife, maybe a police car's on the way. I say, 'There's a video camera, up there.' 'So what?' he says. 'It's evidence,' I say. 'Evidence,' he says. 'What does that prove?' I don't know what's going on in the schools these days. 'Lick my boots,' he says. I'm getting hot under the collar here. I open up the jacket and show him the gun. 'If you don't fuck off,' I say, 'I'll blow your brains out.' 'That's not a gun,' he says. 'Do you think I'm stupid? Lick my boots, loser; you must have a pretty shitty job to be only carrying thirty quid.' When you're dealing with

213

ignorance, you've got to put your foot down right away. Never be reasonable. If it had been a pro, he would have taken my money and disappeared, no hard feelings. I'd've been happy to lose the money. This turd couldn't flush a goldfish down a toilet, and I've serviced dozens of people, but I'm taking the shit. Anyway I'm concentrating hard on being reasonable and law-abiding when his friend, who's a couple of years older and quite hefty, kicks me in the balls. They take the gun. I'm lying there in agony and this old lady toddles past with her shopping basket and I'm thinking, Why doesn't she do something? So the fifteen-year-old takes the gun and fires off two rounds. 'Blanks. It's one of those starting pistols,' he says. In fact, he put two rounds through the windscreen of the police car which was half a mile down the road. The police stop and dive for cover. Then, he puts the gun to his head. Pulls the trigger. There is justice, I think. But the gun's empty of course. So I have to lick his boot while he discusses with his mate which pub they'll go to."

"You don't have any regrets about what you do?"

"Not really. I'm only a shortcut to death. It's not as if I'm denying people immortality. Just trimming a few years off."

"More than a few here."

"Come on, you're what thirty . . . thirty-two? You've had the best. It's pretty much downhill from here. Tits are on the long journey south. You'll end up going to bed with fat accountants 'cause you won't get anything else. This is all an illusion . . . and I'm saving you from the less enjoyable parts. Really, I'm doing you a favor. So do you support a football team by any chance?"

"No. Keen on football are you?"

"That's a tough question. I support Manchester United, but I can't say that makes me keen on football."

"Oh?"

"Yes, you see, I think a real lover of football wants to see . . . football: skill, pace, excitement, drama. All I want is for United to win every match they play ten–nil. It wouldn't even bother me if the other team didn't turn up. Every week, it wouldn't bother me. I want them to beat every team in the world, again and again. Ten–nil. I want some flying saucer to land and turn out eleven tentacled fuckers in an Alpha Centauri strip, and I'd like United to stuff them: ten–nil. I want them to be the greatest football team in the history of the cosmos. I want all history to be dwarfed by the magnificence of their achievement. When people think of Manchester United, I want them to think ten–nil."

"So you go and see them play regularly?"

"No. I've never watched a match. I don't even like to find out the results much."

"How come?"

"Because I get upset when they lose." Dramatically, his pulse, dawdling along at sixty-nine, shoots up to one hundred. "I get upset and I do mean upset." One hundred twenty. He punches the wall several times in a manner that would inflict severe pain on his hand; he picks up a chair and demolishes it. One hundred twenty-two. He gasps: "Ties don't do much for me either." One hundred two.

Perfection. The ideal ideal. A perfection to be part of. Or not even a part of.

"I've thought about taking out some of the opposition's players, but whoever heard of a young, rich, healthy, and famous fucker killing himself?"

"Wouldn't it be ironic?"

"No. It would be implausible. And too many people interested in sniffing around. You bump off an accountant, no one really cares. They've got a few bob, but not enough to really excite. Their partners aren't worried, because they're usually

215

the ones paying me to do it. The families don't give a shit because they've still got the money without the boredom. New threads, nice holidays, more space around the house, fewer arguments about what's on television.

"No, you drop a star player, there'd be rummaging around. Managers, coaches, agents, fans. Besides I've plenty to do, but God, I'm tempted. Especially when there's only a point or two in the championship. And some of the refs."

He makes Nikki roll onto her front and, arching herself to his instructions, she clasps the back of her legs. He places some sugar cubes on her, presumably making her into an approximation of a bowl.

"I always ask people who they support, just in case I come across any Fulham supporters. I'm not very nice to them."

"How come?"

"I was on a train once when this arsehole who supported Fulham got on the train. He was the biggest arsehole I've ever met in my life. I would have brought my professional capabilities to bear, but the train was packed with police. I had to put up with his singing and bad jokes for two hours. Listen, I need something personal of yours, something unpricey, untraceable—a pair of earrings?"

Rosa walks in.

"You're supposed to be in Birmingham," Annihilator says, waving the gun freely.

"I felt ill," says Rosa. It takes Rosa a moment to absorb what is contained in her flat and to fix on Ann's gun and ascertain that it is not an elaborate sexual practice of Nikki's but another hired killer. If Rosa is disappointed to see another simplification in progress, Nikki is more disappointed to see Rosa and not Lump.

"You're probably right: Better to be dead than in Birmingham, but it's messy, messy for me. All right," he

216

commands in the third most used phrase in man-woman relations, a stalwart timewaster: "Get your clothes off." The thing about hired killers is that they're not very nice, and you certainly don't want them in your home.

He looks at Nikki. "Well, it's getting to that time . . . you've got five minutes before I do the business. You know what to do." His pulse: eighty-four. He feels he's getting something in exchange for the trouble. Nikki is finally getting access to Rosa's niceties, but somehow you feel she's not very interested in taking a pussy facial now. Rosa takes off her clothes, ungainfully. A planetful. Nikki, I can see, is tired of playing for time and is going to attack.

The door jumps across the room. In comes Lump. Annihilator is getting jumpy.

"Where have you been?" says Nikki.

"Tea break," says Lump.

"Never mind," says Nikki. "Beat the fuhking shit out of him."

It's all unraveling for Annihilator. He directs the gun toward Lump, who makes no attempt to rush him.

"I told you before. But you wouldn't listen to me, would you?" Lump chides.

"You haven't told me a thing, fatso."

"You shoot me, I win. Shoot me in the head and see what's there."

He shoots into her chest and then, noticing this doesn't alarm her much, one in the head. For the instant before she collapses, light braves the emptiness that has opened in the small circle in her forehead, carrying news of the green wallpaper.

He steps over, curious as to what Lump was talking about. For all her endurance and aloofness to everyday bodily traffic, Lump is now inert, simplified irreversibly, her mission completed. Success? Depends on what the mission was. The gun, I educe is empty, and one on one, I'd bet on Nikki being nastier, not to mention more desperate.

Annihilator is facing me; the girls have their backs to me.

My turn. I don't like to interfere. I grow in a twentieth of a second to eight feet high and six feet wide, and in colors with atomic definition, I show him himself; the one thing no one can look at: his death. He obliges me by losing mastery of his bodily functions; the bodily functions he doesn't want to function function, those he does don't. He reaches one hundred forty-three before he dies, and I revert to the sideboard, looking ceramic.

Rosa sinks to the floor and starts crying. Nikki saunters over to the bodies. "Well, she was right." She stares at Lump's head, seeking clarification. "I need a holiday." She phones for the police, since she obviously doesn't fancy doing any clearing up herself.

The Gorgon vase that was positioned behind Lump has taken two shattering bullets, and the decent-sized shards have been ground into the ground by Lump's mass. Kablooied beyond the redress of glue and patience. Complicated irreversibly. Some sorry fourth-rate provincial museum might offer it sanctuary. Gotcha. I hear, with satisfaction, Nikki's foot crunching another piece. There can't be many of them left. I'm patient. I'll get them. Gorgons, I'm coming for you.

Truthfully, I don't care that much, but I have to convince myself that I do. Without grudges, what would there be to do? Without passions you'd just be sitting on the shelf, ceramicking along.

Djintamoonga and Wopilkara Surprise

She notices Nikki's things are gone.

This time it looks like Nikki's stuff, nothing more.

We've been out to the cottage for a week to recuperate; Rosa knows it's time to hand me over. She's considered buying me up, but she knows that Marius wants me so badly she can't outbid him. No, we're both going to wait for Marius to peg out. Ten? Twenty years? Probably as long as he can hang on, the thought of denying his relatives or anyone else the money rejuvenating; indeed, the notion of being smelly, dreary, and rambling but everyone having to humor him because they want to be showered with money must amuse him. Then, I educe, she'll be waiting to collect me.

Rosa doesn't seem surprised or regretful about Nikki's leaving. One simplifier too many. It will probably be some time before she notices one of her red undergarments is missing, for purposes unknown but not unguessable. Nikki has taken it because we are always fascinated by what resists us and perhaps also because Nikki is savvy enough to know that the imagination can offer us lovers prepared in a way that life cannot.

The auctioneeress arrives, and I am packed away.

"How is it on the romance front?" she asks.

"I'm giving up."

We stop outside as the auctioneeress delves into her purse for her car keys. The auctioneeress can't hear it, but I can perceive the phone ringing in Rosa's flat. It is, I assume, Tabatha, because I hear Rosa say, "I've given up" and "What are you doing at Battersea police station? Posting bail?"

A car has drawn up beside us. It is jammed, front and back, with property. It is the car of someone on the move, eager to bully every inch of space, someone moving into a new flat.

I note zoology textbooks pressed up against the car's windows, heavy, expensive tomes, the frontline texts of a zealot. Reflections on djintamoongas, wopilkaras, and other Australian creatures. Camping gear. Videocassettes. A man springs out with the bounce of a new start. Tall, swarthy, scuba diving, time sweating around in jungles. His hair is black and as rich as an oil jet. A vaulter.

The main reason why Nikki didn't bother lifting any more of the fittings is because she has a tidy sum to travel with, having sold Rosa's flat.

Nikki has gone, her dream at the wheel. The dream is hard to kill. The gleam of a new start is beautiful, the conviction that the future will not be the past is unmurderable for most. Rosa owned her flat entirely and had the deed lying in a drawer. Odd that more people don't try that one. The assumption is that if you're selling a flat, it's yours to sell. Rosa, being conveniently absent for so long, allowed Nikki to be Rosa for her. The check has surely cleared by now, and Nikki is off to unpay more bills, to take perhaps a turn from betraying to be betrayed in her turn.

Prognostication: She will return to Market Harborough and close the circle, ending up in the last place she expected. The back of Market Harborough is farthest away from its front.

The vaulter's hair and brow is indubitably that of the Mop, the lips are those of the painter's daughter. They made it after all. It is also, I suspect, the face I saw fuzzily in Rosa's memory. He soars up the steps and opens the door with what was Nikki's set of keys; I educe from his sports bag that he has a freeze-dried iguana inside. Admittedly not a big one.

As we get in the car, I can just pick up him saying:

"Hello," in a friendly manner, not at all bothered at finding a good-looking woman, vaguely familiar, not wearing a lot, in his flat. You know he's carrying it all. A verbal fragment that allows you to reconstitute everything, a cell from the body perfect. It is a word that has shot her through the heart so quickly, she doesn't realize it's over. Rosa says nothing, no longer surprised or perturbed by anything that enters through her door.

Prognostication: This is the man Rosa will spend the rest of her life arguing with. In time, they will speak of Nikki with fondness, the matchless matchmaker who gave them both a flat worth living in. They will be collaborators on the most chryselephantine pleasure.

Over the years, he will annoy her by being late and then pretending when they arrive that it was Rosa's fault. When Lettuce marries, he will vex Rosa by the stinginess of the wedding present he buys. Rosa's choice of candlesticks will infuriate him, as well as her harshness to spiders.

You know when you're right.

TIBOR FISCHER was born in London in 1959 and educated at Cambridge. He is the author of two previous novels, *The Thought Gang* and *Under the Frog*, which was short-listed for the Booker Prize in 1993, the year he was named by *Granta* one of the "Best Young British Novelists." He lives in London.